CW00857994

# The Turkey Shed

# Gang

## By Ruth Young

First Published in 2022 by Blossom Spring Publishing

The Turkey Shed Gang © 2022 Ruth Young

ISBN 978-1-7396277-4-4

E: admin@blossomspringpublishing.com

W: www.blossomspringpublishing.com

For all my family.

# Chapter 1

Joe was running out of time. He scrambled on the floor looking under his bed, behind it, on top of it. Nothing. He ran his hand along the window sill, threw open the wardrobe door… not there either. Where was his football kit? He was going to be late… again.

'Where is it? Where did I put it?' he mumbled to himself as he chucked his jimjams towards the bed missing it but didn't pick them up. He ran out to the landing and leaned over the bannisters.

'Mum, Mum, where's my football kit?' he shouted down the stairs.

'By the front door in your rucksack where I put it,' called Mum up the stairs.

'Err?' was all could think of saying.

'You should have got up when I told you to,' said Mum walking to the kitchen.

Joe raced down the stairs two at a time and saw his open rucksack by the door with one of his football shirts sticking out of the top. He grabbed the rucksack and a familiar smell wafted up. Mum must have used that awful stuff again when she did the washing. He'd asked her not to use it. Everyone would pick on him again at football this afternoon and say he smelt like a girl.

'Bye,' he called from the open front door, slamming it behind him.

'Have a good day,' Mum shouted from the hall thinking he might hear it. She went back into the kitchen and saw Kit Kat, their tabby cat licking his lips. 'Had your breakfast, Kit Kat?' But Kit Kat didn't answer either.

\*\*\*

Joe trotted along the road to Stewie's house. He pressed the doorbell and it went ding dong. The door flung open and Stewie rushed out his hair wet and his jumper on back to front.

'See you later, Mum,' he called back to his Mum.

'Don't slam the door, Stewie the windows…' came a voice from inside.

Stewie slammed the door shut, the windows rattled as he swung his rucksack over his shoulders.

'Morning, Joe.'

'Morning, Stewie. All right?' said Joe thinking he looked very frazzled — just like yesterday.

'I had to queue up for the bathroom again,' said Stewie, 'and I was last.'

Joe shrugged his shoulders like he did every day. Stewie had three sisters and all they talked about was gel nails, false eyelashes and boys and they drove him mad. Joe was glad he didn't have to put up with anything like that.

'Couldn't wait to get out of there.'

'Come on let's go,' Joe replied.

# Chapter 2

The day got off badly for Joe. Miss Dymchurch, that awful supply teacher who came in sometimes, always asked them to take turns to read to the class. He looked up at her and thought the scarf she tied around her head, made her look like she had ears like a rabbit. He thought she looked funny and then he realised she was looking straight at him. He looked down immediately. He dreaded reading, any kind of reading.

'Right, Joe. Let's begin,' she said glaring down at him from over the top of her glasses.

'Do I have to, Miss?' he asked looking up pleading with her not to get him to read in front of everyone. She never remembered he had trouble with reading. He knew what would happen before it did.

'Get on with it, Joe. We are all waiting,' Miss Dymchurch replied walking around the classroom her heels clicking on the floor making sure everyone was listening.

'S-a-m and the d-u-g w-acked to the daddock,' he read. What he just read didn't make any sense. Whoever wrote this book must be bonkers.

Miss Dymchurch rolled her eyes, 'Joe, it says, "Sam and the dog walked to the paddock."'

The class erupted into laughter. Joe felt his face grow redder and redder and his freckles sizzled. His heart was pumping and he wished the ground would open up and gobble him down. Why couldn't he read? Why did the teachers make him? It always ended up like this.

'What's he talking about, Miss?' laughed Wayne.

'Don't be so cruel,' said Vicky. 'He can't help being bad at reading. Lots of people are.'

'He's fick, Miss,' said Fergus. 'Fick as two short planks.'

'No, he isn't,' said Stewie shouted across the classroom. 'He's got dyslexia, Miss. It means you find reading hard. You all shut up. You're all the dopey ones not Joe.'

Fergus threw his rubber at Stewie and Stewie threw it back. It crashed into Cheryl's bunches and knocked off the hair clip. It spun across the floor.

'Look what you've done you dimwit,' she cried as she scrambled down trying to retrieve it from under the table.

Miss Dymchurch rolled her eyes again and said,

'Will you all stop it this minute? Come on, Joe. Carry on.'

Joe took a deep breath. A croak came out so he coughed and continued.

'A c-a-t  r-a-n in and  bum-ped pu on the f – e – n – k.'

The whole class fell about laughing again.

'No, Joe. It says, "A cat ran in and jumped up on the fence." Are you trying to be funny?' said Miss Dymchurch.

'No,' Joe replied honestly.

Everyone started laughing again.

'I think you had better carry on Laura,' said Miss Dymchurch. 'Be quiet all of you. Joe, you had better see me after class. I do not take kindly to silly little boys pretending they can't read.'

Joe looked down at the book. He wished he was clever like the others. He tried his best to read but the words looked funny when he looked at them and they kept changing shape. One minute it looked like a 'b' and the next it turned itself into a 'd'. Just like magic. The only thing the teachers said he was good at was clearing up after art and craft on Friday. He seemed to be hopeless at everything else.

# Chapter 3

After Science, it was football. Joe had counted down the seconds until it was time to get changed. Footballers don't have to read they just have to be good at kicking balls and he was pretty good at that. One day he was going to be a striker for Man U and that way he would show everyone that he was good at something.

Mr Paige, the new PE teacher, stood in front of the class. His was wearing his Chelsea Football Club tracksuit with the blue lion emblem on the front. Joe recognised it straight away.

'Afternoon everyone. I am Mr Paige, remember?'

Everyone said, 'Yes, Sir.'

Then Kevin said, 'Are you a Chelsea supporter?'

'I am,' he said holding his arms out wide, 'I tried out for Chelsea when I was a lad. I am proud to wear this.'

Everyone looked at everyone else. Tyrone piped up from the back…

'Didn't they take you on, Sir?'

'No, that's why I'm stuck with you lot.'

'But at least you got to a trial,' said Gregory.

'You're right! Not everyone gets to the trials. Now let's see some great ball skills today. I've seen some great playing in this class. Let's have Joe as centre midfield for the reds and Stewie, you go in as centre midfield for the blues.'

The game began when Mr Paige blew the whistle. Blues against the reds.

Joe got the ball and did a terrific pass up the field, Terry dribbled it and passed it to Mikey then the blues got control and everyone ran down towards their goal. The ball went up the pitch and back down again. Then Jonny kicked the ball to Stewie who passed it on to Tiger but Joe intercepted and got control. He ran with the ball as fast as he could keeping it close, dodging the defenders. He had a clear run at the goal he could see Ben, the goalie, getting ready to stop the shot that he was going to...

This was it. This was his **BIG** chance to score. He'd be in the team on Saturday... He continued with the ball as fast as he could, took aim and with all his strength kicked the ball aiming at the top left-hand corner of the net. Ben, the goalie, didn't move. He watched as the ball arched and clipped the post. Why didn't try to save it? It hit the back of the net.

What a shot! What a goal! For the first time in his life, he had actually scored a goal and not just any old goal, a brilliant one just like a professional player for Man U. Joe threw his arms up in the air.

'Amazing,' he yelled dancing around so happy he thought his lungs would burst. He waited for the rest of the team to come and pounce on him and tell him he was brilliant just like the professional players do. But no one came. Everyone stood still. He stopped. Why was everyone in his team glaring at him with their hands on their hips?

'You scored in the wrong goal, you thicko,' said Kevin who was in the A team for the school and always bossed everyone about in lessons.

'We've lost now because of you, Joe,' said Mikey. 'Thanks a lot. Don't pass to him again you lot.'

'That will do, Mikey. We all make mistakes even you do sometimes. Joe, you ran the wrong way,' said Mr Paige. 'Do you know your right from your left, son?'

'I do sometimes, but not always,' replied Joe his head down in shame.

'You need to check which way you're going me lad. Just make sure you look and check next time,' said Mr Paige blowing his whistle.

The game carried on. Joe's knobbly knees were shaking. Next time the ball came near him he went to kick it and missed. He'd volunteer for goalie next lesson. Being a striker was too difficult with too much responsibility. You have to remember that after half time your goal is up the other end.

# Chapter 4

After school, Joe trudged with his heavy rucksack towards home. Stewie had to meet his mum because he had to go to the dentist, so he'd said good bye to him on the corner and carried on alone glad he didn't have to go to the dentist too. That would have been the last straw on an awful day. He sometimes went to Granny Sal's for tea and he did his homework at hers. She lived across the road but he'd decided he wouldn't go tonight as he had so much homework to do. She always kept him talking and he'd never get it all done. He didn't feel like doing it anyway. It would take him ten times as long as all the others in his class and then it would be covered in green crossings out when he got it back from Miss Dymchurch. What was the point doing it anyway?

He was nearly home, when he heard a familiar voice calling him from across the street. He looked up and saw Granny Sal's head sticking out of the front bedroom window. He could see her purple curly hair escaping from the knitted hat she always wore. Her cheeks looked bright pink like she'd been running and her lips were covered in lashings of deep red, glittery lipstick. A cigarette was dangling from her mouth as usual.

'Hello, Joe. How's my favourite grandson?'

'Don't ask,' Joe called up at the window. 'And anyway,

Granny Sal, I must be your favourite because I'm your *only* grandson.'

'Come in and have a cuppa. You look worn out. I've got the kettle on.'

Joe crossed the road and by then Granny Sal had opened the front door. He stomped in and dumped his rucksack on the hall floor.

'What's the matter?' asked Granny Sal as she ruffled his spiky black hair which sprung back like it always did and planted a big, wet lipsticky kiss on his left cheek. 'Had a bad day?'

'Awful, worst ever,' said Joe rubbing his left cheek to remove the bright red lips Gran would've left there.

'That good, eh?' said Granny Sal.

'I read all the wrong words and everyone laughed at me then I scored an own goal because I forgot which end to shoot in. You know what I'm like with my lefts and rights. Gran it was so bad.'

'Never you mind. We all make mistakes. Even the Man U players do. Nobody's perfect. Come on let's have that cuppa. I bought some chocolate éclairs today when I went to the shops. Bought them specially for you, I did. Eat the lot if you like.'

'Thanks Gran,' said Joe sitting down at the kitchen table.

Joe took an éclair from the box. He bit into it. Chocolate

and cream oozed into his mouth and tasted so yummy; he licked his lips to make sure he didn't miss a bit. He took a second one and a third but refused a fourth when Granny Sal held the box up to him again. He sipped the tea and felt better. Out of nowhere, he heard a noise. He thought it was coming from the garden so he looked out of the window but he couldn't see out as Granny Sal's net curtains got in the way.

'What was that?' he asked.

'It's Mr Percival,' answered Gran filling her cup with tea for a fourth time.

'Who's Mr Percival?'

'He's a… now what was the word?'

'Is he the plumber fixing the leaky tap at last?'

'No, silly he's a bird,' said Granny Sal. 'I just can't remember… that reminds me I must phone the plumber. That drip is getting worse. Thanks for reminding me, Joe.'

Mr Percival squawked again.

'That sounds like a pterodactyl. I saw a video last week at school about them. They used to squawk like that when they flew around. Ever so dangerous they were.'

'I don't think he's a "terror what's his name",' said Gran. 'He seems quite a nice sort of fellow actually.'

'A pterodactyl is a prehistorical bird, Gran. They lived ages ago, about when you were little. You know when the dinosaurs were roaming around eating stuff. I learned about it at school.'

'Well, I never. You are such a clever boy knowing all those things, Joe. The man who brought him round didn't say he was a t, t, t, — one of them birds from ages ago, though.'

'I suppose he could be an archeopteryx.'

'I don't think he said that word either. Sounds horrible it does, Joe. Like something you walk in and wished you hadn't. He's a parrot and a sort of unusual one from somewhere faraway like. I can't remember but it sounded like it was a long, long way off from here. It was a funny place I'd never heard of it. That's why I can't remember what the man said when he dropped Mr Percival around.'

'It may be Papua New Guinea. It's near Australia. We learnt about that place in geography,' said Joe.

'You must be a genius, Joe. You know about lots of stuff.'

Joe smiled. Granny Sal always said the right things, made him feel better she did.

'Can I see him?'

'Course you can. Go and say "hello" to him. He belonged to Edna Taggett at number 42. Remember her? She was a dear old soul she was. Lived to 93. Pity about the whiskers and the wooden leg. She did suffer you know.'

Joe nodded. He knew her. He'd often seen her walking along the road with a limp, but he didn't know she owned a parrot or had a wooden leg. She must have always worn trousers or disguised it by some other means because he never noticed it. He'd liked to have seen how the wooden leg worked. She must have had it ages because he didn't think they had them nowadays.

'She passed away last week and she left Mr Percival to me. I really don't know why. I never liked him much. I said 'hello' to him once and that must be the reason. I'm going to sell him on eBay. He's no trouble really, but I'm too old to look after a great big bird like him. The man said all he needs is his food and water and pop him in the cage at night and put the cover over him so he can go to sleepy bye, byes. Remember, I used to say that to you when you were a little bundle of joy.'

'I do remember, Gran but I'm a bit too old for all that stuff now. I am nearly nine remember?'

'Oh, I do, Joe. Quite a young man you are nowadays.'

Joe liked the idea of being a "young man" at last. Being a boy seemed to be going on for a long time if he thought about it. Joe felt his chin to see if any hairs had started to sprout yet. He was going to grow one of those long beards like some of the footballers had. He thought they looked really cool. But the more he rubbed, the smoother his chin felt. No beard yet today, maybe the hairs would come tomorrow…

'So, I'm "bird sitting" until I find him a good home. Someone must want him because I'm certain I don't, so I'm going to sell him. Mrs Golden at number 57 says you can sell anything on eBay, even birds.'

# Chapter 5

Joe got up and went into the dining room. Standing on a metal perch inside a cage with the door wide open, was a magnificent, very big white bird with several bright yellow feather sticking out of the top of his head. His big grey scaly feet ended in menacingly sharp claws which were wrapped around the metal bar. He looked at Joe with his beady black eyes, opened his magnificent black beak stuck out his big, black tongue and said,

'Shiver me timbers. Looks like a squall is-a-coming.'

'Gran he's big,' called Joe.

'He's a big parrot, Joe.'

'I know he's a parrot but what sort is he?'

'I haven't got a clue, Joe. The man told me but I can't remember what he said.'

'I'll look him up in Granddad's bird book. The one we used to look at. You know, before he died. Just a minute I'll go and get it.'

Joe found the bird book in the book case and flicked through the pages. There, on page 89, he found a picture of a bird just like Mr Percival. He tried to read what it said underneath the picture.

'He's a — s-u-l-p-h-ur cr-est-ed co-ck-a-boo from — I can't read that one, Gran.' He pointed to the word.

'S-u-l-a-w-e-s-ee I never heard of it, Joe. I wonder where it is?' said Gran. 'I don't think I've heard of a bird called a cucka what-did-you-say? And that place.'

'It's probably a long way away because I don't think you find them in the trees around here,' said Joe.

'Edna said her husband, Mr Taggett bought him off some bloke down the market. He talks and everything. He sings too.'

'I'm not sure I like him that much,' said Joe. 'He's got shifty eyes.'

Gran left and Mr Percival swung backwards and forwards and the perch creaked as he did it. And all the time he never took his eyes off Joe which made him a bit uneasy. He put the book back on the shelf and went back into the kitchen. Gran was putting the cups in the fridge.

'No, Gran. They don't go in there. Let me take them for you.' He took the tea cups and put them on the draining board by the sink. Gran was forgetting again, getting confused.

'That's better, Gran. I'll wash them up for you in a minute.'

Joe looked at Gran. She had been doing some funny things recently. She had gone out and got lost twice and each time Police Constable Briggs had had to bring her home. She said she had just forgotten what she'd gone out for and got all muddled up and didn't have a clue where she was. Then she left the gas on again — he'd found it on when he got back from school loads of times. Then she set the fire alarm off twice when the frying pan caught fire and the fire brigade turned up. The nice fireman had warned Joe's mum the second time, that Gran needed looking after otherwise she would burn the house down.

'Joe, are you any good at counting?' asked Granny Sal.

'Not really, Gran but it doesn't matter because you don't need to be good at maths to be a striker for Man U do you.'

'No of course you don't,' replied Gran laughing. 'Joe, I've got something to show you.'

# Chapter 6

Granny Sal walked down the hall and Joe followed her. She stopped at a room she called "the parlour" which was "very special". Joe only went in there when it was an important occasion like his birthday or Christmas. He thought this must be one of those "very special" occasions when Gran opened the door and walked in. Joe sniffed... yes, the funny smell was still in there. Mum said was moth balls... and there wasn't even a telly. It was comfy room with two squashy sofas and there was a cupboard with all sorts of glass vases and pottery animals and other stuff on top. Granny Sal called them her "treasures". Normally, Granny Sal spent most of her time in the kitchen because it was the nearest place to the kettle and she drank more tea than anyone Joe knew.

Gran struggled down on the floor onto her creaky knees holding onto the arm of a chair and did a big sigh. She pushed the coffee table to one side and lifted off the rug and put it next to the table.

'This was where Granddad used to keep all his money, Joe. He always said it was safer in here than in any old bank. I never thought it was a good idea meself.'

She grabbed hold of a huge metal ring attached to one of the floorboards and heaved a wooden hatch in the floor up. He saw her lift out a plastic carrier bag from M&S. She opened the bag wide. Gran looked at Joe. He looked inside. It was full of fifty-pound notes.

'Where did you get that from? Did you steal it?' laughed Joe.

'Yes, I think I must have done because when I got home, I had this money in this shopping bag. And I haven't got a clue where it's come from. So, I thought I better hide it.'

'Oh,' said Joe his heart starting to race. He looked at Granny Sal. He needed answers.

'You see, I've had a bit of a funny old day, Joe. I went into town as I needed a bit of shopping and afterwards, I popped into the bank to take some money out my account like I do every Wednesday.'

'Right,' said Joe wishing she would get to the point, not mentioning that today was Tuesday.

'Well, there I was in the queue at the bank chatting to this old bloke about the weather and he was saying that it was very cold for this time of the year and I had to agree with him. It has been very chilly hasn't it, Joe?'

'Yes, Gran.'

'Well, I was still in the queue when all of a sudden, these two men came running into the bank. They had those green rubber monster masks on you know the ones that are covered in warts with the long hair. Horrible they are.'

'Yes, I know what you mean,' said Joe getting impatient.

'Well, they had guns, Joe.'

'Guns?' Joe was wishing he had been there to see the action.

'They shouted at everyone to lie face down but I could hardly get down because of my poor old knees. I told one of the robbers about my arthritis but he told me to "shut it". Well, I struggled down in the end and lay on my tummy. The smell of the carpet was horrible, Joe. And it was dirty too. I don't know who they get to do the cleaning but they don't do a good job.'

'It doesn't matter about the carpet, Gran. Go on what happened then,' said Joe trying to hurry her up.

'The two bank ladies had their hands up. The robbers gave one of the ladies behind the counter, big black bin bags to fill up with money. She took the bag and stuffed it with money and then got the other lady to open her till and then she took all that too. I could see her out of the corner of my eye. When all the money was taken out of everyone's tills, they pointed the guns at us. The robbers snatched the money and ran out of the bank. Then the police arrived in their cars and the sirens were going off and the alarms were ringing. It all went quiet, then this nice policeman helped me up and I told him all about my arthritis. Then I picked up my handbag and my M&S shopping bag and when I got home, I found this lot. I think I must have picked up someone else's bag.'

'But Gran how did you do that?' said Joe in disbelief. 'Didn't you check it was yours?'

'It was right next to me and it looked the same as my shopping bag. I think it might belong to the old bloke in front of me in the queue,' said Granny Sal with a sigh. 'He must have had the same shopping bag as me. Well, I came home and my first thought was I better put this money somewhere safe, so I thought I could put it in Granddad's secret place.'

At that moment Joe heard the blips on the radio. The news bulletin was starting...

*'Earlier today, at ten thirty, two robbers, wearing monster masks, stormed the Western Bank in Handby. The robbers entered the bank and pointed guns at everyone while the staff filled bin bags with money from their tills. Mr Arnold Accrington, sixty-five, of 2b The High Street, who was delivering his life savings to the bank in a M&S carrier bag, has made a statement to the police saying his money had also gone missing. The robbers escaped in a stolen car driven by another accomplice. P.C. Williamson and P.C. Singh helped all the customers and the staff. Now the police believe the robbers may have had an accomplice inside the bank, who police believe was an elderly woman who took Mr Accrington's bag and disappeared. Police are now searching for a woman in her sixties who was wearing a coat and hat*

*— and the two masked men and the get-a-way driver. Anyone with information should contact Handby Police on 016999 275890.'*

# Chapter 7

Joe looked at Granny Sal. 'Looks like you're a wanted woman, Gran,' said Joe.

'Yes, it does, Joe. What shall we do, lovey?'

'I don't know. Give me a minute to think. How much money is there Gran?'

'I'm not sure Joe,' she answered, 'I haven't counted it. Well, it's not mine is it. I don't want to touch it.'

Joe picked one bundle up and removed the rubber band that was holding the notes together.

'Five and five is ten and so you add a zero and that makes one hundred and two more make two hundred,' said Joe and then he stopped trying to count all the notes. 'Well, it's loads, Gran. There must be nearly a million quid here.'

'A million quid? Oh, my giddy heart, Joe. I wish Granddad was here. He would know what to do.'

'Gran, I think we better try and give the money back. We'll say it was a mistake. That you've been getting a bit forgetful lately and you thought it was your shopping bag. You just picked up the wrong bag after the raid.'

'Can't do that Joe; they would never believe me. They'd throw me in the nick and forget about me, Joe. The police are looking for me now. They just said it on the radio.'

'No, they wouldn't. They'd be pleased to have it back I'm

sure they would.' But then he remembered something he'd seen on this show on the telly.

'I'm not too sure, Joe.'

'No, you might be right, Gran. I saw this programme on the telly. There was this bloke and he was innocent but he got the blame and ended up in prison. The detective got it all wrong.'

Joe quite fancied himself as a detective. He could wear dark sunglasses with the mirrors on the front. If the scout from Man U did not spot him at the football trials, he might consider being a detective. He fancied saying, "you're charged with first degree murder", like the guy on the telly. But thinking about things seriously there was a real chance they would *not* believe Gran's story. His little old Gran had, by mistake, stolen a million pounds. She had just picked up a bag full of cash and calmly walked off with it. Now who would believe a story like that?

'No, Gran,' said Joe trying to think straight. 'Look, no one could think you did it on purpose. I'll phone the police and tell them what happened. They are bound to understand.'

'If you're sure, Joe.'

'Yes, I am, Gran. Then we can give the money back. It will be fine.'

Joe went into the dining room and picked up the phone. He pressed 9,9,9 on the key pad. A lady answered,

'Which service would you like?'

'The police please,' said Joe.

'Just one second. Connecting you…'

There was a tremendous crash in the kitchen. Joe threw the phone down on the sideboard and ran into the kitchen to see what was happening. Mr Percival jumped down off his perch and stuck his head through the cage door and picked up the phone with his sharp claws and held it up to his ear.

'This is the police service. How can I help you?'

'A pirate went to sea, sea, sea,' squawked Mr Percival

'Pardon,' said the policeman, 'can you repeat that?'

'To see what he could see, see, see,' carried on Mr Percival.

'Are you trying to be funny?' asked the bewildered policeman.

'But all that he could see, see, see'

'I'm afraid you are not making any sense,' said the policeman again.

'Was the bottom of the deep blue sea, sea, sea.'

'What are you going on about?' asked the policeman getting cross now.

Mr Percival squawked very loudly into the phone, 'Edna, Edna.'

'Sorry, Joe, I dropped the tin of baked beans,' said Granny Sal, 'made a terrible noise didn't it.'

'That's all right Gran. I thought you'd hurt yourself.'

Joe picked up the tin and put it on the worktop and ran back to the dining room. He could see Mr Percival with the phone in his claws.

'What are you doing,' he said, 'give me the phone.'

Mr Percival dropped the phone and Joe picked it up.

'Edna, Edna,' squawked Mr Percival.

'Hello this is Joe,' he said into the phone, 'sorry about that.'

'Are you trying to be funny?' said a man's voice.

'No,' said Joe.

'Is there an adult there I can speak to. I can't get any sense out of…'

'No, you can't Mum's still at work. She doesn't get home until six thirty that is why I am at my Gran's house and she gone a bit, you know, dotty.'

'Who was I talking to just then? They were saying a load of drivel.'

'That was Mr Percival,' Joe replied.

'Can I speak to him again, please?' Said the policeman.

'But he's a parrot,' said Joe wondering why he would want to speak to him again.

'A parrot? And who may I ask owns the parrot.'

'Mrs Taggett did.'

'Put her on the line. I want to speak to her,' said the

policeman.

'You can't, she's dead.'

'She's dead?'

'Yes, she is. She left the parrot to my Gran in her will and now Gran wants to sell him on eBay.'

'You are wasting police time with all this nonsense. Now put the phone down and don't ring us again unless you have an emergency.'

Thinking the money was not exactly an emergency Joe said, 'Okay, I'll put the phone down but could I just mention that my Gran…'

'Now listen here. I have told you that nothing you can tell me is of any interest so please put the phone down,' said the policeman.

'Sorry for the trouble but you see…'

All Joe heard was a click and the line went dead.

'Are the police coming to get the money?' asked Granny Sal.

'No, they told me to stop wasting police time. They wouldn't let me tell them about the money. It was Mr Percival's fault. He was talking to the policeman,' said Joe.

'I wonder what he said?' laughed Granny Sal.

'So, what about the money?' asked Joe.

'What money's that?' said Granny Sal.

'The money that doesn't belong to you,' said Joe realising

that Granny Sal really was becoming *very* forgetful. She had forgotten about the money already.

'Oh, that money. Yes, Granddad used to keep his money under the rug in the sitting room.'

'Yes, I know he did, but what about the money that doesn't belong to you? The money from the bank raid,' said Joe.

'Oh, *that money* well I suppose I had better put it back under the rug in Granddad's hiding place.'

A newsreader interrupted the music on the radio.


*'There is an update on today's bank raid in the town. Police are searching for the robbers who raided the bank **and** the M&S carrier bag containing the missing money belonging to Mr Accrington. The raid was carried out at Western Bank on the High Street. Police are searching for an elderly woman, who the police believe was the robber's accomplice. She took a bag belonging to a man in the queue who was trying to pay in his life savings. The woman, we repeat, the woman, police are searching for is in her sixties and was wearing a matching coat and a knitted hat. Anyone with any information…'*

# Chapter 8

'We'll have to go on the run,' said Joe standing up and taking charge. 'There's nothing else we can do,' he said firmly.

'But what about school, Joe?' asked Gran thinking straight.

'School? I can't go to school Gran.'

'On the run, Joe? I've never been on the run before.'

'Neither have I, but there's always a first time for everything. Come on, we can't waste time. The police will have got you on CCTV so we have to go now.'

'Shall I leave a note for Mum, Joe? She'll need to know where we are, otherwise, she'll call the police.'

'Yeah, you're right, but I'll write it. I'll leave a note saying an old school friend of yours in say — Scotland — has taken a turn for the worse and I had to help you get to see her before, you know, she kicks the bucket. Yeah, that's it. That's a great story. She'll think we've gone to Scotland but we'll be going the opposite way. We'll be going to... the Isle of Gull. We can go and stay in Granddad's caravan. No one will think of looking for us there. We haven't been for ages.'

'Sunny Ridge Caravan Park. Now where did I put the keys to the caravan? I think I put them in the drawer. Hang on while I have a look.'

Granny Sal tottered off to the kitchen and tugged at the

knob to open the drawer under the kettle and rummaged around. She took piles of papers out, followed by bits of string, old tea strainers and measuring tapes. Then right at the back of the drawer she spotted a set of keys with a 'Have Good Day' key ring attached to them.

'Here they are Joe. The keys to "Tropical Sunset."'

'Tropical Sunset?' asked Joe. 'What's Tropical Sunset?'

'That's the name of the caravan. Granddad called it "Tropical Sunset" because it reminded him of the tropical sunsets over the horizon when he was a mechanic on the cruise boats. All those exotic places and all that funny food and people who say things and you haven't got a clue what they're going on about. You know Joe, he would be really proud of you. You know the way you look after Mum and me.'

Joe blushed bright red.

'You can get there by train and then the ferry, Joe. But it's November so the caravan park won't be open.'

'I know, Gran. That's the whole idea. We can lay low in the caravan until this all blows over. So come on, there's no time to keep chatting now. I'll write the note, you pack a bag. Best get a hat and a pair of sunglasses to, Gran.'

'Is it sunny today, Joe?'

'No Gran, it's November. The sun does not shine in November, does it? No, we need a disguise.'

'Good idea Joe. What would I do without you?' said Gran as she gave him a big lipsticky kiss on both cheeks. 'Joe, did you know those continentals always kiss on both cheeks,' she continued with a giggle.

'There's no time for all that stuff, Gran. You've told me a million, no, a trillion times about the way that lot kiss, now get a move on. We have cops to lose.'

# Chapter 9

Joe ran back over the street and unlocked his front door with the key, which was attached to a piece of string he had around his neck. He ran into the kitchen and tugged at the drawer where Mum kept the sticky notes and pulled the pad out and a biro.

*'Helow Mum, Gon to Scootlard whith grany sal to see her frend Effel woh is gonner kik the buket. Be baek in a foow days. Downt worree wil fome yu. See ya. Joe. P.S. Hop you had a god daye.'*

Joe looked at the note. It was covered in blotches and some, no most of the words, looked a bit wrong but he was not sure which ones. He knew Mum would be able to read it and he didn't have time to worry about that now. He ran into the hall and stuck the sticky note on the mirror which was just by the front door. He knew Mum would see it as she always looked at herself to check her hair was not sticking up and her mascara was not smudged when she got home.

Joe ran upstairs and opened his wardrobe. Inside he found his best jeans, the ones Mum bought in the charity shop in the town last time she went shopping, along with tartan shirt and a pair of socks with stars and stripes on them. He found a plastic carrier bag under the bed and stuffed them in. He jumped back downstairs two steps at a time and grabbed his fleece hanging on a row of pegs by the door, thinking that would be a good idea. He slammed the door behind him and ran back over to Gran's.

'Gran, Gran,' he said rushing through the door.

'In the kitchen dear. I thought we'd have a nice cup of tea before we set off. Do you want two sugars or three? I can't remember what you like. I don't know what I did two minutes ago! I think it must be old age, Joe.'

'What are you doing?' said Joe out of breath. 'We may only have minutes before the cops come knocking at the door. We don't have time for a cuppa. We've got to get out of here NOW.'

'Oh Joe, you know I am no use unless I have a cuppa. I can't get my head around things without a cup of builder's.'

Gran poured out two cups of steaming tea into two thick mugs with smudgy flowers painted on them. Granny Sal handed him a mug. 'Biscuit?'

'Gran, have you packed a bag?'

'No, not yet dear,' she said.

'Now drink that up quickly and go and pack.'

'It'll be nice having a little holiday won't it. I haven't been to the seaside for ages. Last time was when I went with the pensioners group. We went on a coach and it was lovely but it didn't stop raining all day...'

'Gran. Now. Go and pack a bag.'

'Pack a bag. Righty oh, Joe. Will I need my bathing suit?'

'It's November, Gran.'

'Oh, so it is. I won't bother with it then.'

'Just some warm clothes and — a toothbrush,' said Joe remembering that he had forgotten his.

Gran struggled upstairs and Joe went into the front room and picked up the shopping bag of money and placed it carefully back under the floor. He fixed the hatch firmly back in place and lay the rug over the top. Then just to be sure he moved the coffee table back to where it was and pulled Gran's favourite chair on the rug too, to disguise where the money was hidden. He heard the stairs creak and then a thud. He walked out into the hall. Gran's arms were laden with clothes. She had her blue winter coat on and her matching furry hat with the purple ribbon. She dumped everything in her shopping trolley and did up the zip.

'Is that everything, Gran?'

'Yes, Joe. I think I've got all I need.'

'Have you turned the gas off and locked the back door?'

'Not yet, Joe. I'll go and do that now.'

'I'll do it.'

'Thank you, Joe.'

Joe put the empty tea cups in the bowl and checked the

gas was off and pulled out the kettle's plug from the wall. He turned the key in the back door and hung it up on the hook on the wall next to the curtains. He ran upstairs and checked the windows in the bedrooms. Everything looked closed so he ran down the stairs two at a time.

'Right, we're off.'

'Yes, we are, Joe. Come on Mr Percival,' said Gran as she picked up the parrot cage and dragged her shopping trolley through the front door.

'Gran, we can't take Mr Percival. We have to travel light.'

'Joe, I can't leave him behind. There's nobody to look after him. I mean who would fill up his water and food bowl? Mum won't, she's always hated birds. Always been terrified of them she has. I think she had some problem when she was a little toddler. She always talks about this budgerigar who flew at her. Now where that budgerigar came from, goodness knows. I don't ever remember anyone having one and I certainly don't remember one flying at her.'

'Oh, come on then,' said Joe as he opened the door and nudged Gran out.

# Chapter 10

Granny Sal tugged the trolley along and with one hand and held onto Mr Percival's cage in the other, Joe followed closely behind. A niggling thought crept into his head. Was this a good idea? Ever since dad had run off with the barmaid from the Dog and Duck pub when he was six, he'd taken on the role of Mum's and Granny Sal's protector. He had learned over the last two years to be "the man of the house" as Mum called him. This was a very important job and he didn't mind doing it. But he did have to make important decisions sometimes and take control. Since Gran had been forgetting things, he found his job getting more and more demanding. He'd mentioned it to Mum and all she'd said Gran was old and that's what happened when you got old. Now he wasn't so sure.

Trouble was, it was very hard to say "no" to Granny Sal who was so kind to him. She was always ready gave him a fiver for weeding the garden or making her a cup of tea and she always bought him just what he wanted for birthdays and Christmas especially if Mum said he couldn't have them — like his *Ripster Board* and his *GraviTrax Obstacle Starter Set*. Gran always whispered she had a bit of money saved from renting out the caravan and Granddad had left her a bit too so there was no reason not to spoil him. She also had her pension which she collected every Wednesday from the bank. She didn't spend much only some on her fags which she bought from that nice Mr Patel in the Post Office down Market Street.

Joe and Gran continued down the road. The shopping trolley rattled along the pavement as Granny Sal dragged it behind her. Mr Percival was still swinging on his perch enjoying being outside — he very rarely ever went out in the fresh air these days since Mrs Taggett died.

The tram stop was at the end of the street just before the traffic lights. The tram went all over the town and ended up at the station.

'Evening Mrs Brookwood,' waved Gran in the direction of Mrs Brookwood's curtains which suddenly fell back with a swish. 'She's a nosey old coot that one, Joe. She knows everyone's business in the street.'

'Gran, don't say anything and don't look at anyone. We don't want them saying to the police they saw us walking down the road. Come on,' said Joe speeding up to nearly a jog.

They waited at the tram stop. Joe stood on tip toes to look at the timetable to see what time the next tram was due but as he did, he saw the lights of the tram in the distance coming down the street.

'It's coming, Gran. Have you got your tram pass?'

'Yes, here it is, Joe. Can you take it for me? Here's twenty pence for your fare, Joe. You'll need a single child's fare.'

'I know, Gran,' said Joe. She seemed to have forgotten they took the tram every Friday after school to do the weekly shop at the out-of-town supermarket on the by-pass.

'Single to the station please,' Joe asked the driver, 'and this is my Gran's pass.'

'Thanks son,' said the driver.

Joe lifted the trolley onto the bus and Gran huffed and puffed her way along the aisle with Mr Percival still swinging on his perch and plonked herself down on a seat with him on her lap.

'Hello,' he squawked to the surprised passengers. 'I'm Mr Percival.'

'Can't you shut him up, Gran. Everyone's looking,' said Joe.

'Shush now, Mr Percival. There's a good boy. Sorry everyone,' continued Gran. 'My friend's husband, Mr Taggett bought him off a man in the market. He must have taught him to speak. He comes from somewhere foreign. What was it called, Joe?'

Joe, looked out of the window. Now they all knew his name. He wished he had remembered his beanie hat and wore it as a disguise. He pretended not to hear.

'Funny thing to buy in the market but he loved the bird.

Of course, poor old Bert Taggett has passed away long since now and his wife too just last week. That's why I've got him. She left him…''

'Gran, please shut up. No one is interested. Sit down and don't say anything.'

'Joe, I think I've remembered something,' said Granny Sal into his ear.

'What have you remembered Gran?' said Joe.

'Now let me think. It was something to do with, you know,' she said looking around, 'the money but I can't quite remember. It was something to do with Granddad. If I don't write things down, I forget them.'

'Shut up, Gran. Don't say a word about the money.'

# Chapter 11

The tram rattled along the tracks. By some miracle Mr Percival stopped talking. Joe sat down and put the plastic shopping bag at his feet and his rucksack on his lap. He twiddled the toggle on the zip nervously. It was then he noticed a police car pulling up at the traffic lights next to the tram. He nudged Gran and winked and looked the other way.

'Gran, it's the police. Look down, don't look out of the window,' he whispered.

'Which window?' whispered Gran.

'This one,' said Joe pointing to the window next to Gran with his thumb.

Gran looked straight out of the window and said, 'This one Joe?'

'Don't look now, Gran. They might see us.'

'And we don't want that now do we,' said Gran. 'Don't look out Mr Percival. Joe will tell us off.'

The traffic lights went green and the police car sped away. Joe sighed and his breath clouded up the window. That was a close shave. To be that near to the police when you are on the run was nerve racking. He could feel his heart thumping in his chest. Joe willed the tram to go faster and eventually, after ages, he heard the driver say,

'Next stop the station. Don't forget to take all your

possessions with you. Thank you for using the tram today. See you again soon.'

'What a nice man, Joe. Lovely service. Thank you, driver,' she called in the direction of the driver as she got off the tram.

'Come on Gran. We have a train to catch.'

Joe went up to the ticket office and had to stand on his tip toes again to reach the counter. If only he had listened to Mum and gone to bed earlier these past few months. She had scolded him nearly every night about going to bed so late.

'If you go to bed early then you'll grow, Joe. I heard it on the telly. Young boys can't grow unless they get a good night's sleep.'

He had gone, 'Mum, you know you can't believe everything you hear on those stupid programmes. They talk a lot of rubbish.'

Now he wished he had listened to her. He wished he was a few centimetres taller and then he could reach above the counter and look a bit older.

'What can I do for you young man?' asked the man at the counter.

'Single child to Sandport and a single pensioner ticket too, please,' he asked in his deepest voice. He knew how to lower it because Mrs O'Nuff, the drama teacher, had shown him how to do it for the Nativity play last Christmas. Mrs O'Nuff said he was very convincing in rehearsals so he added that success to his list of achievements. But all hadn't gone to plan on the first night. As he walked out centre stage to say his lines, he lowered his chin, like Mrs O'Nuff said to make his voice go lower, but some of the hairs on his false beard stuck up his nose and made him do the biggest sneeze and the beard flew off his face and skidded across the stage. He didn't know what to do. Should he get it or just leave it where it was? The audience started to titter, then laugh and point at him. Mrs O'Nuff glowered from the wings. Joe puffed out his chest, lowered his beardless chin right down and said in a great big booming voice,

'Whoopsadaisy!' He turned to the audience and cleared his throat. 'Well, I didn't think that would happen... Oh yes, and there's no room in the inn. We are very busy and all the rooms are taken. But you can have the stable. Come this way.'

Joe waved at Mary and Joseph to follow him off the stage. The audience had started to clap, some stood up, some wolf whistled. Afterwards he got lots of praise for his performance as everyone said he gave the funniest innkeeper they had seen in years and that he had managed to get some humour into the same old play they did every year...

'That will be twenty pounds and five pence my lad,' said the man.

Joe handed over a twenty-pound note from his pocket that Gran had given him. He fumbled in his pocket for a five pence piece.

'What are you looking for Joe?' asked Granny Sal.

'Five pence. Have you got one?' asked Joe.

'Pieces of eight, pieces of eight,' squawked Mr Percival.

Joe felt his face flush bright red. 'Keep him quiet,' he hissed at Granny Sal.

Granny Sal opened up her big, red handbag with a snap. She emptied out all the contents on the counter. There was her diary, purse, at least ten old shopping lists, a lipstick and her gold powder compact with the embroidery back, a packet of fruit pastilles, two leaky biros and a half-eaten ham sandwich in a box which had green mould on the edge and her cigarettes and Nicorette gum because she was trying, not very hard, to give up smoking.

'I'm sure I've got one of those little five pence pieces in the bottom here somewhere. They're so small I can't pick them up. I broke my nail last week when I was weeding the garden and I have had nothing but trouble ever since. Look at it,' she said holding it up for Joe to see.

From behind a voice said,

'Can you please hurry up; I'm trying to catch the five-thirty to Crigton.'

Joe turned around and saw a queue of people behind them

all muttering to each other and getting impatient.

'Gran, have you got one? We are causing a scene,' whispered Joe.

'There it is. Joe, can you get it out for me. It's there down in the corner. Look there it is. Did I tell you about my nail?'

'Yes, Gran you just did. Now everyone in the queue knows my name, Gran. Shhh. Let me have a look.'

Joe spotted the five pence coin in the corner of her bag and scooped it up. He handed it to the man who gave him the two tickets.

'The next train is at five forty, platform three.'

'Thank you,' said Joe in is deepest voice and not forgetting his manners. He knew if he did not say thank you Mum would go off on one of her rants if she heard he had forgotten.

Gran put everything back in her handbag, lifted up Mr Percival and dragged the trolley behind her. There was a round of applause from behind as the queue filtered forward to buy their tickets and run for their trains.

# Chapter 12

The train pulled into the station and the squeal of breaks resounded on the platform. Joe pushed the button on the door when it flashed green and beeped, and the doors opened with a swish. Granny Sal heaved herself and Mr Percival up onto the train. Joe lifted the shopping trolley up and Gran carried on down the aisle to find some seats. They found a three-seater together and Gran sat down with Mr Percival in the middle. Joe put the bags on the luggage rack and plonked himself down. He did a big sigh.

'This is your guard speaking. This train is for Sunnyport. We will be stopping at Warmindale, Bortham and Chaplam. Refreshments will be served from the buffet cart. Everyone must have a ticket. If you do not you will have to pay the full fare plus a penalty fare. I will be passing through the train shortly to check your tickets so please have them ready. I would like to take this opportunity to wish you a very pleasant journey.'

Joe patted his anorak making sure he had the tickets safe inside the secret pocket with a zip. He had snatched them away from the ticket office counter in case Granny Sal took them as he didn't trust her to keep them safe. A lady reading her book suddenly looked up and saw Mr Percival. Joe saw him wink at her. The lady's eyes widened.

'You're a bit of all right,' he squawked.

'Well really,' said the lady taking her glasses off. 'Should you have a parrot in the train where there are passengers? He looks dangerous.'

Granny Sal and Joe looked at the woman.

'He's just a naughty boy aren't you, Mr Percival. He's not dangerous at all. Just ignore him. He won't do you any harm.'

'Fancy a walk under the stars and the moon?' squawked Mr Percival.

'Shut up,' said Joe to Mr Percival.

'That parrot is a menace,' said the woman standing up.

'Sorry, love. You see, when Mr Taggett bought him in the market he already knew how to speak. He's ever so clever. He can sing too,' said Granny Sal to the lady.

'I have no interest in the background of that tatty old bird,' tutted the lady.

'Mrs Taggett,' she whispered with a wink, 'has left him to me in her will. She died just last week. Not too keen on him myself. But he's an orphan. Got no one in the world now, so until I can sell him on eBay, I'm looking after him. Now I have a daughter and a grandson and a parrot. Joe's mum is a lovely girl. Bit neurotic, but lovely all the same. She hates birds too, like you.'

'That's all very well,' continued the lady, 'but has he got a ticket? I'm going to get the guard. I am not going to sit here listening to him going on about the moon and the stars and waffling on about nothing of interest to me.'

The lady got up with a huff and stormed off.

'Can't we cover him over and he might go to sleep,' suggested Joe.

'That's a good idea Joe. What could we use? I should have brought his night-time cover. I never gave it a thought,' said Granny Sal.

Joe went over to the shopping trolley in the luggage rack and dug his hands deep inside. He felt something large and soft and tugged. It was a pair of Granny Sal's enormous knickers. They were pink and baggy with long legs that fitted down to her knees with elastic around the bottom. He pulled them out and looked at Gran.

'That's a pair of my pantaloons. If there isn't anything else they'll have to do.'

Joe zipped up the shopping trolley again and went back over to Granny Sal. She took the pantaloons and stretched the elastic on the waistband and pulled it over the top of the cage and pulled them down so they fitted snugly down covering him. Joe tied the legs together at the top so they didn't flap about. Suddenly Mr Percival gave a great, big sigh and said,

'Good night.'

'That will keep him quiet at least now, Gran. We were

trying not to bring attention to ourselves and now look what's happened.'

The door between the carriages opened with a swish and in came the guard with a flourish. He stood and looked at Joe and Granny Sal like an army Sergeant Major surveying his troops. He cleared his throat. His eyes fixed on a round contraption covered with a pair of pink knickers. He cleared his throat again.

'Tickets please,' said the guard.

Joe took the tickets out and handed them to the guard.

'Have you got a ticket for that?' asked the guard.

'No, we didn't think we needed one for Mr Percival,' said Granny Sal.

'Who is Mr Percival?' asked the guard.

'He's the foul-mouthed parrot,' said the lady from behind the guard.

'He's a poor little orphaned parrot,' whispered Granny Sal, 'thinks he's a person though. Been in the Taggett family for years. He's in the cage asleep.'

'I'm awake. Get me out of here,' came a voice from under the knickers. 'Help, help. There be a squall a-coming. All hands-on deck.'

'What did I tell you,' said the lady. 'They have got a mad parrot in a cage. He should be in the baggage hold. Animals shouldn't be allowed to travel where there are people.'

'Is that a parrot in there?' asked the guard.

'Yes,' answered Joe. This was a nightmare. There he was thinking they could be incognito and now the whole compartment, no, probably the whole train, knew about them and Mr Percival. This did not happen on those police programmes on the telly.

'Let me see what is under those,' said the guard lowering his voice, 'under-garments.'

Granny Sal pulled up the legs of her knickers and they lifted off the cage. Mr Percival started to swing on his perch.

'The wheels on the bus go round and round...' he squawked.

'Shut up,' said Joe.

'Be quiet there's a good boy,' said Granny Sal kindly knowing this was how to get the best results from such a bad tempered, ill-mannered parrot.

'Right, no ticket, no seat. He'll have to go in the baggage compartment,' said the guard.

'I should think so,' said the lady as she settled herself down in the seat.

Joe got up and picked up the cage.

'I've got a lovely bunch of coconuts,' said Mr Percival.

'Shut up,' said Joe, 'we don't want to know about your coconuts.'

# Chapter 13

Joe's mum, Marilyn, was on the forty-two-bus going home. It had been a long day. All that hard work for very little money but it was better than nothing and to be honest, she quite liked the job even though it was tiring. She had done the cleaning at Doctor Trumpington's, the retired doctor, this morning in his great big house. She had sat with Mrs Trumpington and had a cup of tea and a biscuit as they talked about the weather. When she left, she went to the park and ate the cheese sandwiches she made this morning for her lunch as it was a lovely day. She had sat on a bench in the sunshine, even though it was chilly, sharing them with the pigeons. She always threw them some crumbs and when she was finished, put the newspaper wrapper in the bin. She liked to think she was an eco-friendly warrior. She recycled everything she could and always did the right thing to save the planet. After she cleaned Mrs Wong's house, the nice lady who owned the Wing Wah Chinese take-away on the High Street, she had popped into town to the market and bought some carrots, tomatoes and broccoli that were going cheap at the end of the day. She would add them to some baked beans which would make a lovely tea for Joe who was always starving. It was one of his favourite dinners which was lucky because money was short and she had to do what she could on just a few pounds a day.

Marilyn got off the bus and walked in the direction of home. It was a bitterly cold now and foggy. She never liked November. Such a cold, miserable month. She glanced at her watch. It was six thirty. She hoped Joe was doing his homework at Gran's but as she walked past Gran's house it looked deserted as there were no lights on. They must have gone to their house. She wondered why. Perhaps Joe had wanted to do his homework at home for a change. Yes, that was it. She only hoped Gran didn't complain about the lack of meat in tonight's dinner. Gran could never understand why anyone wanted to be a vegetarian.

Marilyn had also noticed recently that Granny Sal was getting very forgetful. She kept repeating herself and forgetting where she had put things. She knew Joe had noticed too and she had explained to him, at the time, that it was all part of getting old. But she had seen programmes on the telly about old people getting so dotty they had to be taken into a home. It was becoming a real problem everywhere she had learned with an "ageing population". Granny Sal was getting on, there was no denying that, so she'd keep an eye out in case it got worse and tell Joe to as well.

Marilyn let herself in through the front door of the house. She called out Joe's name and no one answered. The hall was dark so she switched on the light and called again. Still, no one answered. She noticed her reflection in the mirror and checked herself and was pleased she still looked tidy, and that's when she saw Joe's sticky note. She picked it off reading it carefully trying to decode Joe's terrible writing and even worse spelling. She really must buy him one of those self-help books for spelling next time she went shopping. Joe's teacher had said at the last Parent's Evening that Joe needed extra help and they would try to get him some. In the meantime, she tried to help him with Friday's spellings but he found them so hard like she did. The government cutbacks were hitting everyone hard, and that included Joe.

With difficulty, Marilyn managed work out what Joe's note meant. What was Joe thinking of? She had told him he must never bunk off school. She wanted him to make something of himself. Not like her who had mucked about at school being the class clown because, like Joe, she had found learning really hard and the teachers always made her feel stupid. Her friends had called her 'thick' and made fun of her. She could never remember the long lists of spellings she had to learn on Friday for a test on Monday, either like Joe. In the end she had given up and left school as soon as she could. She had never really mastered reading. She could read simple stuff but reading books took too long. She always lost the meaning half way through the sentence. She had no proper qualifications. How could you have them when you could not even read the questions in the exam? She wanted better for Joe. She knew nowadays there was help out there. Problem was it cost money and she did not have a great deal of that.

Marilyn's first thought was to phone the police. She read the note again. Joe was a sensible boy. He would keep in touch. He would phone she knew he would. She filled the kettle to make a cup of tea but she felt uneasy. It was unlike Granny Sal to do something like this. She had never heard of a friend called Ethel. She really could not remember her ever mentioning someone with that name and certainly could not remember her talking about anyone who lived in Scotland.

Marilyn ran upstairs and opened Joe's bedroom door. She looked in the wardrobe. There were two empty hangers on the rail. He must have taken the jeans and nice tartan shirt with him. She ran back downstairs and saw that his fleece was not on the peg in the hall. She grabbed her coat and Granny Sal's key and ran over the road.

Granny Sal's house was cold and dark. She pushed open the kitchen door. That awful parrot, Mr Percival was gone too. Her shopping trolley, which always sat by the front door, was also missing. There was only one thing to assume. That the two of them really had gone to Scotland to see this Ethel who was seriously ill and about to die. She slammed the door behind her and ran back over the road. The kettle had boiled. The little red light on the phone light was *not* flashing to say there was a message, so no one had called yet. Her mobile phone didn't flash up a message to tell her there was a text or a missed call. She made a cup of tea and sat down in the kitchen. She stared at the phones willing them to ring. The more she looked at them the more they stayed silent. She would have a lot to say to her mother when she spoke to her and she would have even more to say to Joe. How could he be so naughty as to go off on some jaunt with his grandmother in the middle of November? What was he thinking about? Then an awful thought struck her. Perhaps Granny Sal had got confused and thought she had a friend in Scotland and Joe tried to stop her and realised he had no option but to stay with her. She knew he took on the role of "man-of-the-house" very seriously. She knew she relied on him too much. He was only a boy after all. How could she have been so silly as to not see this sort of thing could happen.

Marilyn looked over at the T.V. There, on top, was a photo of Joe and Granny Sal. It had been taken in the park last summer. Joe's skinny legs were crossed as he sat on the grass. His black spiky hair, which was cut very short, was standing to attention like it always did. His freckly face beamed with happiness. Granny Sal was sitting on a deck chair wearing a wide brimmed straw hat with a bunch of grapes on the front. It was such a happy picture and she always smiled when she looked at it. They were the "Inseparable Duo" the best of friends. Joe would never let his granny go all the way to Scotland on her own.

'Oh, Joe where are you? Where have you gone? What has happened to you?' she said aloud and her voice seemed to echo around the room.

Then a thought crossed her mind. Perhaps she better phone the police just to be sure. They could intercept them on the way to Scotland but she had no idea how long they had gone. She remembered the police waited some time before they told you to worry if someone went missing. No, she would wait for a call first from Joe, and tell him to come straight back home and they would all go to Scotland together.

# Chapter 14

Granny Sal and Joe took Mr Percival to the baggage compartment and placed him down in the corner.

'I think we better cover him over again,' said Joe as he pulled Gran's pantaloons down over the cage once more. 'You go back and sit down and I'll stay here and keep an eye on him. Someone might steal him. I bet birds like him cost a load. When I go back to school, I'll Google it to see what he's worth. Maybe £300?'

'Never, Joe. Three hundred smackers for a bird like Mr Percival? Mr Taggett must have wanted him very badly to pay that much for a bird. I can think of lots of things I'd rather buy with that much money.'

'I'll come and find you just before we get to Chaplam. It's the stop before Sandport where we get off for the ferry. You go back in the warm carriage. I'll be fine out here,' said Joe.

Joe sat on a suitcase and looked out of the window. It was raining quite heavily now and rivers of rain water wriggled their way down the window looking like worms. It was cold too in the baggage compartment as it was not heated like the carriage. He wished he thought to put on a jumper under his fleece *and* his school anorak. There is never enough time to pack when you are on the run, he must make a list just in case he ever had to do it again.

'The next stop is Warmingdale. Please remember to take all your belongings with you when you leave the train. Thank you for travelling with Country Rail today. We hope to see you soon,' said the guard through the train's loud speaker.

The train ground to a juddering halt and Joe could hear the doors swishing open. He could hear rattling as people dragged their luggage down the platform. Then everything went quiet. Joe looked at his watch. He could see 18:35 in big red numbers. He loved his watch because it was like the ones that pilots wore. At least that's what Granny Sal told him. She had got it in the market and the stall holder had assured her that the captains on Jumbo jets wore these watches because they needed to know what the time was all over the world at that exact moment. It had a dial on the side that you could flick up or down. Each flick was an hour forwards or backwards. It must be very handy if you were a pilot, Joe supposed, but of course he had never needed to put the time forwards or backwards apart from twice a year when the clocks changed.

He had seen an advert on the telly about holidays and there had been a pilot on it. Joe liked the look of the uniform. All those silver stripes and a big, black bag and a cap. He had gone to the airport once when his mum was meeting an old school friend, who was coming home from her holidays. He had seen a pilot walking through the terminal and saw everyone looking admiringly at him as he strutted along. That was really cool. Being a pilot must be very important and very exciting. Flying to all those places that you see on those programmes on BBC2 that he sometimes watched with Mum. He fancied visiting those places. He decided that if he wasn't chosen as a Man U apprentice, or be a detective, perhaps being a pilot was a good alternative. He'd look up, 'How to be a pilot' on *Google* when he got home. If it meant he would have to work harder at his spellings and reading he would, to have an exciting job like flying great, big aeroplanes.

Joe was feeling really hungry wishing he'd packed some sweets out of the box Mum hid on top of the kitchen cupboard. She kept them up high so *she* didn't eat them all at once. She climbed up on a chair took two for Joe and two for her after dinner every evening. It was such an effort, all that climbing and risky too, but it stopped her doing it more often. Joe could have climbed up to get a few if he'd thought about it. He didn't think he'd be hungry at the time after all the chocolate eclairs at Gran's. Of course, he had never had to run away from the police before, so it had never entered his head. He would know better next time. Then he stopped himself. What was he thinking of? He would NEVER run away again. Then he thought he was only running away now to protect Granny Sal. Who would have thought that running away would need careful planning? And the responsibility? It was mind blowing when he thought about it.

The door to the baggage compartment swished open and two policemen walked in. Joe's heart stopped. His felt his face heat up. As quickly as he could, he slithered down off the suitcase he was sitting on onto the floor and turned to face the wall.

# Chapter 15

'Right George, you go forwards and I'll go to the rear of the train. They've got to be here somewhere,' said one policeman, 'there was a positive sighting by a member of the public.'

'I'll keep in close contact, Colin,' replied George.

They must have been rumbled, thought Joe. Mum must have called the police and now they were on the wanted list. Joe had watched an old black and white cowboy movie with Granny Sal one wet afternoon when he was off school with a cold. The sheriff had put "Wanted Dead or Alive" posters up all over the town with the faces of the outlaws on them. His face and Granny Sal's must be up all over the towns already. They would be all over social media and the News on the telly. And *Crimewatch* too. He could see it now. There would be a lady standing next to their picture saying they were dangerous thieves who stole money from some old bloke in the bank. There would be CCTV footage of Gran in the raid. Everyone must know. Anyone could recognise them and hand them into the police. This situation was bad and it was becoming even more serious.

As the policemen left, Joe quickly and quietly as he could, picked up Mr Percival's cage and crept towards the door back in the direction of Granny Sal's carriage. He could see one policeman on the other side of the door talking to some passengers and he was busy so he could slip past. He reached up and pressed the button to open the door.

'You all right there, son?' asked the other policeman who appeared behind him. Joe nearly jumped out of his skin and did not wait to answer him. As the door swished open, he dashed through it and ran to Granny Sal.

'The police are here and they are looking for us,' spluttered Joe as he shook Granny Sal who had fallen asleep. Granny Sal woke with a start.

'Are we there, Joe?' asked Granny Sal. Her unlit cigarette smeared in bright red lipstick and hanging off her bottom lip moved up and down as she spoke.

'No, the police are looking for us Gran. They're on the train.'

'Who is on the train? Joe I was just thinking a minute ago about the bank. You see I remembered...'

'Gran, you've got to get up. The police are looking for us,' said Joe looking behind him expecting the policeman to come up to him any second.

'All right, Joe. The journey went very quickly, didn't it? I'll just get the shopping trolley. Help me up, will you?'

'The police are down there,' Joe whispered, 'they're onto us.'

'The police, Joe? Looking for us? Oh, my Lord. What

shall we do?'

'Follow me,' whispered Joe and he grabbed his rucksack and slung it over his shoulder, picked up his carrier bag and Mr Percival's cage and headed for the front of the train away from the police officers.

'The train is just approaching Bortham. Passengers, please remember to take all your belongings with you. Thank you for travelling with Country Rail today and we hope you will travel with us again soon,' said the guard.

'That's lucky we're stopping. Come on we'll have to get off here and try to get to Sandport on a later train,' said Joe.

Granny Sal collected the shopping trolley as she went past the luggage rack. The train squealed to a halt and when the green light shone out on the door button, Joe quickly pressed it and the doors sprung open. It was dark on the platform and Joe noticed a light over a door ahead of them. There was a "toilet" sign on the door.

'Come on quickly we'll hide in here. The police will get off the train to see if we have got off too.'

Joe tried to push the door open but it was locked. Ahead he could see the two police officers walking along the platform outside the train. He had to think quickly. This could be it. The game may be up.

'I be starving,' said Mr Percival from under Granny Sal's knickers.

'Shut up... now!' Joe said and rattled the cage. Mr Percival got the message and shut up.

Joe looked frantically around. 'Come on, Gran. We'll walk out of the gate. Make it look like we know where we're going.'

Joe started walking. Granny Sal followed. He glanced back. He could see the police officers talking to the guard. Then the guard said goodbye and the police got back on the train. The guard blew his whistle and the train pulled away.

'That was close Gran. We've done it; we've given them the slip. Now we all we have to do is get the next train to Chaplam and hope there are no police on board.'

'Any remaining passengers please make your way out of the station now. That was the last train tonight. The station will reopen at six o'clock in the morning for the first train of the day,' said the station guard. As the guard finished speaking the lights on the station went off with a click and they were suddenly standing in complete blackness.

'Oh, dear Joe. What shall we do now?' asked Granny Sal looking around at the empty station.

'I'm not too sure,' said Joe. 'But we can't stay here. Let's get out of here and walk to the town. We might find a pub or a café. Come on.'

Granny Sal followed Joe out of the station. There were some lights at the far end of the road up a hill. They set off,

Gran pulling the trolley which bumped along the cobbled stones and the perch squeaked as Mr Percival swung backwards and forwards. It was very quiet. There was no one about and no cars going down the street either. Joe was worried about Granny Sal. She looked very tired as she dragged the shopping trolley behind her.

'Look, Granny Sal there's a pub. Let's ask them if they do rooms for the night. That would help. They might even do food.'

'Good idea Joe. I'm a bit tired and I could do with a cup of tea. Bet you're hungry love,' she added.

'Yeah, I'm starved. Mr Percival must be too. I hope they don't mind pets,' said Joe as an afterthought.

'No one minds Mr Percival,' said Granny Sal.

A squawk came from the cage followed by, 'Shiver me timbers.'

'Mr Percival, stop you naughty boy,' laughed Granny Sal.

'Yo, ho, ho and a bottle of rum,' sang Mr Percival at the top of his voice.

'Shhh,' said Joe. 'Shut up, you'll have us all in the nick and then what'll we do?'

# Chapter 16

The door of the pub was slightly ajar so Joe pushed it open. Inside was warm and bright. A huge fire burned in the grate and there were people drinking and playing darts and cards. Music blared out from a juke box in the corner. There were tables and chairs in what looked like a restaurant to the side. A waitress was serving dinner to a lady and a man. Granny Sal followed Joe up to the bar.

'Good evening, Sir,' said Joe. 'I was wondering if you could help me. My gran would like a cup of tea and we'd like something to eat if possible. My gran has money in her purse to pay.'

'Good evening, young man. I'm afraid you can't be in here. This is a pub. You're not fourteen, are you?'

'No, I'm not,' replied Joe.

'Best you go into the restaurant. I'll get Tracey to help you. Tracey, look after these people, will you?' called the man behind the bar.

A young waitress with blond hair piled high on top of her head waved to them to come forward. Joe looked at Granny Sal and the two of them walked towards the welcoming restaurant. It was good to be inside where it was warm. Granny Sal sat down at the table they were taken to by Tracey.

'Can I get you a drink?' she asked fiddling with the earring on the side of her nose.

'I'd love a cup of tea please and what do you want Joe?' asked Granny Sal.

'I'll have a coke please,' asked Joe.

'Here are some menus. We've got a delicious steak and onion pie tonight or there's fish and chips. Look there's the specials board over there too,' pointed Tracey to the wall. 'There's spotty dick for pudding with custard or ice cream if you prefer or apple pie.'

Joe was so hungry he almost said he would have everything. Tracey left and he and Granny Sal studied the menu. He looked at all the words and tried to sound them out. St... eee...k and ch...o...ps. He was not sure what steek was so better avoid that. Sc...am...pi and sal...ad.... what was scampi? It sounded like some sort of stuff like liver or guts. It was taking too long to work out all the words and even when he worked them out, he was not sure what they were anyway. Mum never cooked anything like these things ever and Granny Sal only did fish fingers and sausages, ordinary stuff like that, not this fancy stuff.

'I'm having the steak and onion pie, Joe. I love pastry and spotty dick for pud.'

'I'll have the same Gran,' said Joe relieved that Tracey had told them the thing they liked the best. He looked over at the specials board and there was no way he could even attempt to read the curly writing. It would take him even longer to try and work all those words out.

Tracey returned and took their order. There was a television in the bar and Joe could see it was on. He could only faintly hear the newsreader.

*'They were spotted on the five forty train and the police are in pursuit of the criminals. They are known as the ...'*

Joe stopped listening and watching. They were on the news. He dare not tell Granny Sal he did not know how she would react. He just hoped there were no pictures of them on the telly. If they had pictures, someone in the bar was bound to recognise them. They would stay calm, eat their meal and then go and find somewhere to sleep tonight. Staying in the pub would be too risky. The news reports would be full of sightings of them on the tram and at the station and the train. There was nothing they could do now but stay put. To suddenly get up and not pay for their meal and the drinks would only make matters worse and bring more attention to themselves.

Joe looked nervously around. No one was looking at them. No one was taking any notice of the News. Tracey appeared with a pot of tea for Gran on a little tray with a jug of milk and a bowl of sugar cubes and a glass of coke for him. Joe looked at the glass. His coke had ice and a slice of lemon in it and a bendy straw. He felt like James Bond as he picked up the glass. He'd never had a coke like this before. He'd watched a movie with James Bond in it. He had drinks like this and his chinked too just like his when he drank some. He wondered why James Bond didn't drink beer like Stewie's dad did. Joe wouldn't know which beer to order so perhaps James Bond didn't either. He knew that beer made you a bit squiffy if you drank too much of it. Mum sometimes had a beer mixed with lemonade and when she had two or three of them, she started to talk funny. So maybe James Bond got squiffy too like Mum and then he couldn't fight the baddies. Joe thought it was probably a good idea especially if James, like him and Gran, was ever on the run.

Granny Sal lifted the corner of her pantaloons and opened the little door in Mr Percival's cage. She tipped some bird seed into his bowl from a packet she had in the front pocket of her shopping trolley.

Tracey appeared again with two small round pottery dishes each with the steak and kidney pie inside, on a plate with some peas and chips. Joe sniffed at the delicious smelling steam as it spiralled out of a hole in the top of the brown, flaky pastry. He looked at Gran who was already tucking into hers. They didn't talk, just ate until their plates were clean and they put their knife and fork down. Tracey cleared the plates and came quickly back with two bowls of spotty dick under lashings of thick yellow custard. Again, the smell was delicious and Joe scraped the plate and Gran did too. When they had finished, they both sat back.

'That was absolutely delicious,' said Gran.

'I'm stuffed,' said Joe looking down at his tummy. He could see his tummy sticking out in the gaps in between his shirt buttons.

'Yes, it was very tasty, Joe. What are we going to do now?'

'Gran, we've been on the News on the telly. I think we better go and find somewhere to stay tonight and then we'll get the train tomorrow down to Sandport. Once we get to the caravan, we can lay low and we'll be fine.'

It was then that Joe felt something nudging his trouser legs. He looked under the table and saw some feathers disappearing upwards. He looked up to the seat next to him. Mr Percival settled himself next to him and started pulling out his tatty feathers.

'If you go down to the woods today,' sang Mr Percival at the top of his voice.

Joe looked around and saw everyone in the restaurant was looking at them and laughing.

'You're sure of a big surprise,' continued Mr Percival.

People came in from the bar to see what was going on, murmuring that it was not every day a parrot came into the pub, dogs yes, but a parrot no. And this one could talk as well that was quite something.

'Gran, get him back in the cage. Everyone is looking.'

'I can't have closed the cage door. Come here Mr Percival there's a good boy,' said Granny Sal sweetly.

Unfortunately, Mr Percival had spotted a stuffed duck in a glass case on the mantelpiece above the fire. He jumped down off the chair and stomped over to the fireplace, he hopped up onto a table, which luckily no one was sitting at, then using his beak and his claws, climbed up to the mantle shelf and walked over to the duck. He patted the glass case with his beak.

'Come on, this way to the poop deck,' he said to the duck.

The duck did not move. Mr Percival tapped the case again with his beak.

'Follow me you bilge rat,' he screeched.

The duck still did not move. The crowd of people in the pub all started to laugh and some started to clap. Mr Percival looked up to see his audience. He hung upside down holding on to the edge of the mantelpiece with his claws. He flapped his feathers and splayed out his tail as he swung back and forth.

'Five little ducks went swimming one day,' he squawked

at the top of his voice.

Quickly, Joe got up and dashed over to Mr Percival. He grabbed him with both hands, avoiding his sharp claws and his beak, and shoved him back into the cage. He slammed the door shut, pulled Gran's pantaloons back over the cage and sat back down and caught Tracey's eye and smiled broadly.

'Can we have the bill please?' he asked.

'Sure, no problem,' said Tracey. 'Better get him out of here quickly,' she added, 'before someone phones the health inspectors.'

'Yes, yes of course,' said Joe.

Joe looked about. Everyone had gone back to their seats and weren't looking anymore which was good. But now everyone in the pub had seen them. They would find it difficult to deny it was not them now when they appeared on the News.

Tracey returned with the bill and Granny Sal handed Joe her purse. Joe counted out the money and put it on the saucer that Tracey had left. There should have been a pound change but Joe decided it was not worth waiting for just that, so they stood up, gathered up their belongings and walked out of the pub.

# Chapter 17

Joe and Granny Sal walked up the lane away from the centre of the village. It was bitterly cold and the sky was full of stars sparkling like diamonds as they twinkled. There were very strong country-like smells and Joe guessed they must be near a farm. Sure, enough they came to a large wooden gate. Gran read the sign out loud which said, 'Blackberry Farm'. Through the gate was a barn and the door was ajar. Joe opened the gate and let Granny Sal through and he closed it without a sound. He pushed the big wooden door of the barn and it creaked open. Inside it was cool and dark and smelled of grass and dust.

'Gran we'll have to stay in here tonight. We can sleep up there, look.'

'That's the hayloft. We could climb up there,' said Gran.

'Nobody will find us in here. Looks like everyone in the farm is asleep. It's very dark everywhere so no one will see us. We'll be safe in here,' said Joe.

'We'll be fine, Joe. I used to go apple picking when I was a girl. That was what we did years ago for our summer holiday. We did not have much money then and the only holiday my parents could afford was the train fare down to this farm in the middle of the countryside somewhere. We used to pick the apples all day and then we'd have picnic lunches in the fields and dinners under the stars in the farm yard. Then we'd all sleep in the hayloft. Those were the good old days, Joe. None of those funny foreign places where no one speaks English and they eat slug's feet for dinner covered in that white stuff like an onion. What's it called? Garpic or something like that or is that what you put down the toilet.'

'Gran, it's garlic and they don't eat slug's feet they eat frog's legs,' said Joe.

'Well, whatever,' replied Gran. 'It's all disgusting anyway. Poor little frogs going around all legless. What harm do they do? Nothing, nothing at all. They just swim around the pond minding their own business and then along they come and the next thing their legs are in a casserole boiling up in a great, big pan. Disgusting. I mean how much meat is there on a frog's leg? They are only small little things, frogs. We used to catch them in the pond at the top end of the town near the canal but we never hurt them. I'm sure if we ate frogs' legs and we'd be on the toilet for days, Joe.'

Thinking it best to end this conversation quickly Joe replied, 'Yeah Gran. Can you climb the ladder?' he continued pointing to the hayloft.

'I'll have a go, Joe. Not as young as I used to be. Come on, Mr Percival,' said Gran as she held on to the ladder rung with one hand and nervously put one foot on the ladder. Joe took Mr Percival from her thinking she would need both hands free. He stood at the bottom of the ladder and watched as she went up. When she got to the top, he struggled up with Mr Percival.

Gran lay down and covered herself in straw and so did Joe. There was a little skylight window and Joe could see out into the night sky. The moon appeared from behind some clouds to join stars which continued to twinkle. It was all very pretty even though it was so cold.

'The stars don't look like that at home do they, Gran,' commented Joe.

'No, they don't, Joe. Must be because we're out in the country. Must be lovely to live somewhere like this. No, polluption and noise. No traffic and queues at Tesco's.'

'It's pollution Gran,' corrected Joe. 'Now, if I can't play for Man U or be a detective or a pilot, I'll be a farmer and you, me and Mum will come and live here when I'm grown up. What do you say, Gran?'

'That sounds wonderful, Joe. Granddad always said he would have liked to be a farmer but he was hopeless at growing things and he was scared of cows too.'

'Shiver me timbers,' added Mr Percival.

'And do you know I was only thinking a while ago about Granddad and his savings.'

'What about them Gran?' asked Joe trying to keep awake.

'You know Joe, I can't remember what he did with them in the end. It was something about the bank. Perhaps I'll remember in the morning. Good night love,' said Granny Sal yawning.

'Good night, Gran.'

Joe closed his eyes but he couldn't sleep. Everything that had happened was worrying him. He had to keep Granny Sal from going to prison. He had to do a good job at keeping her safe. He wondered what Stewie would think when he saw his picture on the telly. He'd be shocked. He could imagine him telling the police about his terrible reading and the own goal. He shivered at the thought. He heard Granny Sal's muffled snores so he knew she had already fallen off to sleep. He lifted the pantaloons up a little bit so he could see if Mr Percival was asleep and he could see him motionless on his perch and tucked his head under his wing. And with that, he felt himself drift off to sleep in the soft, warm hay.

In the morning it was the smell that woke him up and the cows mooing nearby. Gran woke up too.

'Doesn't it pong here, Gran.'

'That a real country smell. We don't get smells like these at home, do we?' she laughed as she picked bits of straw out of her hair.

Joe stretched. The smell of grass and fresh cow poo filled the air, he jumped up and looked out of the window. A tractor thumped along the farm road and stopped outside. The farmer got down and was emptying a load of muck making a big heap on the ground. It smelt disgusting. He waved to a lady feeding chickens in an enclosed area. Joe wondered what the time was. Looking at his watch, 7:30 shone out. They would have to sneak out so they would not seen. He did not want to have to explain to the farmer and his wife why they were in their hayloft all night. And they would probably recognise them from the telly… the list of people that could identify them was getting bigger all the time…

# Chapter 18

Marilyn also woke up with a start. She must have just nodded off because she had lain awake for what seemed like the whole night. She had watched the hours click around on the digital clock as she tossed and turned from one side of the bed to the other. At one stage she had given up and gone to make a cup of tea and then gone back to bed to have another try at getting to sleep. Then somewhere around five o'clock, she must have dozed off at last. She glanced at the digital clock and the red numbers said 7:30. If Joe did not phone soon, she would have to call the police. There was nothing else for it. She had waited long enough.

If only she had listened to him when he had asked her for a mobile phone for his birthday. She had said he was too young and they really couldn't afford one and who would he phone anyway? Joe had said that all his friends had mobile phones and you could play games on them as well as phoning people and what would he do if he was attacked by a flock of dragons or fell in a snake pit? He wouldn't have a phone to make an emergency call to the rescue services. She had said, as she looked at his freckly face, that the chances of that were remote and to stop being silly. Now she realised Joe had been right. If he had a phone, she could call him. Now he would have to find a public call box and she knew how difficult it was to find one that worked and had not been vandalised. Everyone had mobile phones nowadays so finding a phone box was like trying to find a needle in a haystack. She was not sure she could even remember seeing one lately. With all the council cuts perhaps, the public phones no longer existed.

Marilyn looked down at herself. She was still in yesterday's clothes. She'd go and make some tea but didn't feel like any toast. She walked down the stairs. Deep down she knew Joe was a sensible boy who could look after himself but he had Gran to look after too and Mr Percival that awful parrot that her Mum had inherited. She would wait until eight and if there was no call, she would ring the police. She filled the kettle and switched it on. Things always seemed better after a cuppa. Cups of tea worked wonders. As she waited for the kettle to boil, she stared at the phone wishing it to ring.

'Joe, please ring me. Let you know you are all right. Please,' she said aloud.

The phone did not ring.

***

Joe and Gran climbed down from the hayloft and walked to the door. He lifted the latch and slowly pulled the door towards him trying to stop the door scraping on the floor of the barn. He stuck his head out.

'Can I help you?' came a voice.

Joe's heart stopped as he saw the farmer staring straight at him just outside the door. He tried to think of an excuse and he could feel his face getting hotter and hotter. Then he heard,

'Breakfast, breakfast. What time do you call this?' squawked Mr Percival.

'That's our parrot,' smiled Joe at the farmer.

'Your parrot? What have you been doing in our barn with a parrot?' said the farmer.

'Well, it is like this... and this,' said Joe pointing to his Gran who had now come out too, 'is my Granny Sal.'

'Excuse me madam but what are doing in my barn with a parrot and a small boy?'

'I'm in your barn with Mr Percival who is my parrot and my dear grandson, Joe,' corrected Granny Sal.

'But why?' asked the farmer scratching his head.

'Um I'm not sure,' answered Granny Sal looking anxiously at Joe. 'Joe I can't seem to remember. Why are we here?'

'Well, it was like this, Sir,' said Joe trying to give himself time to think up an excuse. Why would he be in a barn with his granny in November? 'Well,' he continued, 'we were going to visit some friends and we got lost. Then it got dark so we had to find somewhere to stay so we could carry on today. All your lights were off so we thought you had gone to bed and we did not want to wake you up to ask you if you would mind if we slept in your barn.' He hoped this sounded convincing. His heart was pounding in his chest going boom, boom, boom.

'Did a taxi bring you here then? You don't seem to have a car?' asked the farmer with his arms folded now.

That was a good idea, thought Joe. He would not have thought of that. A taxi of course.

'Yes, we came in a taxi. Granny can't drive,' he replied.

'And where do your friends live?' asked the farmer.

Joe had to think quickly. 'Next to the pub,' he replied. 'We must be off now. Thank you for allowing us to stay in your barn.'

'Yes, of course. Now I remember. There was the bank and the...' said Granny Sal.

'The sun is over the yardarm,' squawked Mr Percival.

'Shhh,' said Joe staring at Granny Sal and winking at her. Trying to distract the farmer he pulled Gran's pantaloons out of his rucksack and dragged them back over the top of the cage. They had to make their escape. He could see the farmer's wife coming to join in. He could see she had a phone in her hand and she was talking to someone. He guessed she was talking to the police. There must have been mug shots of them on the Ten O'clock News last night.

Joe and Granny Sal turned and quickly walked away towards the village.

'What's going on?' asked the farmer's wife.

'No quite sure,' said the farmer scratching his head.

'The feed merchant is on the phone for you.'

The farmer took the phone from his wife and as he did, he said, 'That was funny. That old lady and her grandson and a parrot stayed in our barn last night. Said they lost their way trying to find a house next to the pub.'

'There isn't a house next to the Pig and Whistle, only the village shop and the church,' replied the farmer's wife. 'Did you forget to lock the barn again?'

'Fred? Deliver today? That's fine,' said the farmer.

# Chapter 19

Marilyn picked up the phone and dialled 999. It was 8:05.

'This is the emergency services. Which service do you need?' said the lady on the other end of the phone.

'I need the police,' said Marilyn.

Click, click. 'Police service. How can we help?'

'I want to report two missing persons,' said Marilyn.

'Two missing persons. Right, names,' said the policeman.

'Granny Sal, I mean my mother Sally Grimshaw and my son Joe Dawson,' replied Marilyn. 'Joe left me a note…'

'Your mum and your son? Right when did you last see them? And what did the note say?' continued the policeman.

\*\*\*

Joe and Granny Sal arrived at the station and Joe paid for two single tickets to Sandport. The train was in half an hour so they went to sit on the platform bench.

'I could do with a cup of tea, Joe. I find it hard to get going without my early morning cuppa.'

'I know Gran. There's no cafe here and the pub was closed. I could go to the village shop and get you a can of coke maybe?'

'Oh Joe, I could not drink that stuff. All those bubbles

would go up my nose. No, a cup of tea for me. Do you think they'll be a buffet cart on the train?' asked Gran hopefully.

'There's sure to be one,' said Joe but he was doubtful. They were not that far from the coast from here. The next part of the journey would not take long. The buffet cart maybe closed. He just hoped he was wrong and it would still be serving people. It was the early morning train service so many people would want hot drinks. He looked at poor old Gran was looking very tired. He had noticed she was huffing and puffing a bit more than yesterday as she lugged the trolley behind her. She must be feeling pooped — he was too.

Eventually the train chugged alongside the platform. When the button on the train door flashed green, Joe pushed it and the doors swished open. Granny Sal got on carrying Mr Percival and Joe did too pulling his bag and the shopping trolley behind him.

The guard was standing at the end of the carriage. Granny Sal walked up to him.

'Excuse me young man. Is there a buffet car on the train?' she asked.

'Tickets please,' replied the man.

Joe took the tickets out of the pouch at the front of his rucksack and showed them to the guard. 'Excuse me but is there a buffet cart on the train? My Gran needs a cup of tea,' he said.

The guard looked at the tickets and then he looked slowly at Gran and Joe. Joe started to panic. Perhaps the guard had seen the wanted posters with their pictures. Surely, he would give them up to the police. He would tie them up in the baggage compartment. They would be gagged and bound. The police would stop the train at the next station and they would be arrested and taken to the cells at the local police station. Mum would come and there would be all sorts of trouble and Gran would be thrown into prison and he would end up in a young offender's jail like the boy in EastEnders...

But all he said was, 'Yes, son. We've got a buffet cart. Go that way, three carriages down.' Then he walked away clipping tickets as he went.

Joe and Gran found some free seats together which had a table in the front of them. Gran sipped her tea and from a cardboard cup and ate a bacon roll which she had squirted the whole content of a sachet of tomato ketchup into. Joe was chomping his way through an egg mayonnaise sandwich and drinking coke from the can. It was a bit of a funny breakfast but neither of them cared.

'Years ago, you could go to the buffet car and sit down and have a proper breakfast,' said Gran wiping her mouth with the back of her hand. 'Granddad and I used to go all over on the trains when we were younger. He always treated me to breakfast or lunch in the buffet car. It was a real treat. Nowadays it's all this fast-food stuff.'

'Yes, it is,' said Joe as he popped the last of the crust into his mouth licking his lips so he didn't waste any.

# Chapter 20

Marilyn heard the doorbell and went to see who was there. A lady and a man in police uniform were standing on the doorstep. Marilyn held the door back and they walked into the hall. She took them into the kitchen.

'Would you like a cup of tea?' she asked them.

They nodded and the policeman took out a little notebook and a pencil.

'Right,' said the police lady. 'We need to know all you can tell us. When was the last time you saw them and can we see the note?'

***

The train pulled into Sandport station. Gran and Joe followed the signs for the ferry. Seagulls screeched and swooped making a terrible noise as they squabbled with a greasy chip bag by the side of the path as they walked along. There was a salty smell in the air and a rumble from the ferry's engines. A thin misty drizzle was falling making the whole place look gloomy. If only this had happened in June; the weather would have been better and the sun could easily have been shining and it would have at least been warm.

At the ticket office, Joe bought two ferry tickets for

Clarkson-on-Sea. They would get a taxi from the ferry port to the caravan site once they were over on the island. As they walked down to the boat, Joe passed a telephone box but the phone was dangling limply from its cradle. The wire attached to it was frayed and some of the thin wires inside were snapped off. There was no way that was working. He would make sure he found a phone as soon as he got over to the island and phone Mum. He guessed she would be frantic by now. He just hoped she had not phoned the police yet but he had a nagging doubt in his mind. If only he had made more effort in trying to find a phone box yesterday. If he had spoken to her, he could have convinced her everything was fine.

They followed the signs down to the ferries. Joe kept going until he reached the one that said 'Isle of Gull' and stopped. He looked at the ticket and the letters looked the same on the ticket as the sign so he knew he was at the right one. Granny Sal caught up and together they walked up the ramp to get on board. At the entrance, one of the sailors, wearing dark blue overalls and a white cap, asked for their tickets and Joe rustled in his anorak pocket for them and handed them to the man. He read them and looked at Granny Sal then at Joe. Joe looked down at the ramp floor. The sailor must be thinking he seen them before. He should have told Gran to wear her sun glasses and pull her knitted hat down a bit more but he hadn't thought of it at the time. The man paused again and looked back at the tickets.

'Not a very nice day for a sailing. It might be a bit choppy. All right son, this way.'

Joe did a big sigh and picked up his bag and Mr Percival. The sailor couldn't have seen the News. He didn't know who they were. Joe smiled but didn't make eye contact just to be sure and took back the tickets; the man helped Granny Sal with the trolley pulling it over a hump from the ramp to the boat.

'What's under the pink pantaloons?' the sailor laughed scratching his head.

'Our parrot,' said Joe forcing himself to tell the truth.

'In for, in for me, they've all got it in for me,' said Mr Percival from the cage.

The man laughed again. 'And I'm Long John Silver,' he called after them.

They found some seats by the window and Joe went to buy Granny Sal some more tea and another coke for himself. The lady put some packets of sugar, the coke with a bendy straw sticking out of the lid and a big cardboard cup filled to the top with tea with a plastic lid with a hole in it, on a tray for Joe. He looked at the string with a label attached to the tea bag dangling limply down the side of the cup. Joe knew Gran would not approve of making tea in a cup like this.

She'd say you have to have freshly drawn boiled water, heat the pot and put one tea bag in per person and one for the pot and let it brew for five minutes and use a tea cosy. It was a ritual he had seen her do millions of times.

'Thanks, Joe, for the tea. Tastes like dish water but it's hot and sweet at least,' said Gran as she poured the third packet on sugar into the cup and stirred it round with one of her biros from her handbag.

The sea was quite rough and the boat went up and down with the swell. Joe started to feel a bit queasy and Mr Percival was swinging on his perch, which seemed to make made matters worse.

'Gran, I think I'll have to go up on deck. I feel a bit peculiar,' said Joe.

'Yes, you do look a bit peaky love. You've gone a bit green. Will you be all right on your own?' asked Granny Sal who was sitting very comfortably and really could not face the cold wind out on the deck.

'I'll be fine Gran. You stay in the warm. The journey only takes about forty minutes. We'll be there before we know it.'

'You know there's something about that money that's puzzling me. You see I think…'

'Not now, Gran. We'll talk later.'

Joe walked out onto the deck. The cold air hit him like a sledgehammer. He wished he had brought his woolly hat, gloves and scarf with him. The ones with Man U on them that he wore for football club practise on Sunday mornings in the winter. He leaned on the railing and even though he felt really cold, he started to feel a bit better in the fresh air. Ahead he could see the island. It was not that far at all. They would be there in no time. It was then that he heard two voices behind him.

'Yes, they were seen in the pub and then they disappeared. They must have the money with them. I can't understand why they are not using a car as the getaway vehicle, Sir.'

'Yes, I agree,' came the answer. 'I think this "Turkey Shed Gang" have an approach to keep on the move with public transport. It's odd for a gang like them but so far, they have managed to keep in front of us so their tactics must be working.'

Carefully, Joe glanced around. There were two men in plain clothes talking and Joe guessed they must be police officers. They must be talking about them. But why was he calling them the Turkey Shed Gang? He must have heard them wrong. They were not a gang at all and they certainly did not have anything to do with turkeys. It was all very odd.

Joe tried to work it out... someone in the pub last night must have phoned the police and told them their whereabouts when they recognised them on the News at Ten and

*Crimewatch* — and probably social media. That meant

even people thousands of miles away in Sulaweewongs, or whatever that place was called that Mr Percival came from, knew about them. The people from that place might *even* recognise Mr Percival. He and Gran must be on the wanted list of worldwide criminals. The police name for them was, "The Turkey Shed Gang" for some reason. But they hadn't run off with the money. They'd left the money in Granddad's secret hiding place. Joe wondered if their crime was bad enough to be put in the Tower of London or in a dungeon, like the one he'd seen in that museum he'd been to for his friend Mickey's birthday party. The Chamber of Horrors it was called. The gory wax works made him feel quite woozy. Some of the time he had closed his eyes because he just could not bear looking at the revolting dummies. Luckily it was so dark in there he had got away with his friends not seeing his green face. The experience had given him nightmares for weeks. He knew he could never be a doctor... he could never add *that* job to his list.

Joe sauntered back along the deck and once he went round the corner he darted as quickly as he could back to Granny Sal.

'The police are here. They are definitely onto us Gran,' he said out of breath giving her a nudge because it looked like she had nodded off. Her head was slumped down on her chest. A squashed cigarette was hanging from her bottom lip.

She opened her eyes with a jerk and said,

'There you are, Joe. What did you say? I couldn't quite catch that.'

'The police Gran,' whispered Joe. 'You know, the ones who are following us.'

'Oh yes, dear, that lot. They are a nuisance, aren't they? All we're doing is going on a little holiday and they can't even let us do that. I blame the government. Always interfering in other people's business. You know Joe, I was thinking before I nodded off about Granddad's hole under the floorboards. I think I've remembered...'

'Gran we'll have to be careful getting off the boat so they don't see us. Put your sunglasses on and try to keep Mr Percival quiet. They probably know about him too. I heard them talking about a gang called "turkey something". They maybe don't realise he's a sulper crusting cotapoo or whatever he is — I can't remember the exact name...

'I think it's a sulphur crested cockatoo, Joe. Mrs Taggett always called him one of those. I do remember her saying it all the time.'

Joe wasn't listening. 'That's it. They must think the three of us are in some sort of gang. Mr Percival makes us more conspicuous. There can't be too many people travelling on the ferry with one of them now can there?'

'Yo, ho, ho and a bottle of rum,' said Mr Percival who

was feeling the need to join in.

'Shhhh,' said Joe.

'I'll have a half,' came a reply but he was a quieter this time.

# Chapter 21

The ferry pulled into the docks. Joe and Granny Sal waited until all the other passengers had disembarked and then they gathered up the shopping trolley and the bag and Joe's rucksack and Mr Percival and headed for the way out. There was no one around apart from two sailors smoking by the exit gang plank, so they got off the boat and quickly walked towards the taxi rank. Joe looked about him and saw, way down the jetty in the other direction, the two plain clothes policemen he had seen earlier, talking to policeman in uniform. They were deep in conversation and they were looking in Joe and Granny Sal's direction.

'Quick this way. Don't look around just keep going. There's the taxi sign. Follow me,' said Joe with the deepest voice he could muster. Granny Sal carried on dragging the trolley behind her and it rattled and bounced along the gravel. They joined the queue of people waiting for taxis.

'Joe, I'll be glad to get there won't you? It's such a long time since we had a little holiday,' said Granny Sal with a sigh.

'Gran we're not going on holiday we are going into hiding.'

'Are we? Why are we doing that?'

'Remember,' he said in hushed tones, 'the money?'

'Yes, I've been thinking about that…'

'Not now, Gran. I'll be glad when we get to the caravan,' he replied and continued, 'I'll get the driver to stop at the shops and we'll do some food shopping before we get to the caravan park.'

'You are a sensible boy, Joe. I wouldn't have thought of that. We'll need something for tea. We could get some sarnies couldn't we. We need milk and bread for breakfast and maybe some eggs. That'll be nice. I'll treat you to a pizza in that nice restaurant at the caravan park.'

'The restaurant won't be open, Gran. It's November remember. Nothing will be open. The caravan park only opens in March near Easter and closes in October so we'll be the only ones there. It's a great place to hide out. Come on here's the next taxi,' said Joe as he raised his hand up to the driver and the taxi came to a halt.

'We want to go to the Sunny Bay Caravan Park please,' said Joe.

'No point going there, son. It's closed for the winter,' said the driver.

'We want to go there anyway,' replied Joe. 'We have the keys to our caravan.'

'But you'll freeze to death in your caravan this time of year. That's why it's closed.'

'We'll be fine. It's all sorted,' said Joe using his deepest voice. 'And can you stop at a supermarket on the way please.'

'Will do, if you're sure, son. I'm just a bit concerned for the old lady there. Your Gran, is she?' said the driver.

'She'll be fine. She's got me to look after her,' Joe retorted.

'My grandson is one in a million,' said Granny Sal.

'Ahoy, me hearties,' joined in Mr Percival.

'Shhhh,' said Joe, 'take no notice of him.'

***

The rain was pounding down now and even though it was only three o'clock it seemed like night had already come because it was almost dark. The taxi drew up to the entrance of the Sunny Bay Caravan Park and the big iron gates by the wooden hut, which was the reception office, were closed and padlocked.

'See I told you,' said the driver, 'the whole place is shut up for the winter.'

'It's no problem,' said Joe getting out of the taxi. 'We'll be fine. Don't worry about us.'

'Want me to take you to a hotel? There are a few open down on the front overlooking the sea. There's a nice B and B run by my mate. She'll look after you and it's only thirty quid a night including breakfast. Full English. My mate is a great cook... bacon, egg, sausage, beans, black pudding and fried bread. Nice cup of strong sweet tea?'

'That sounds good, Joe,' said Granny Sal who was now wondering if staying in the caravan in the middle of winter was in fact such a good idea.

'No, we'll be fine,' Joe repeated as he opened the door of the taxi and scooted around to open the door for Granny Sal. Then the taxi driver lifted up the boot and took out the shopping bags and dumped them on the ground.

'Here you are son. This is my number. Call me if I can help you. That will be fourteen pounds please,' said the taxi driver handing Joe his card.

Joe took the driver's business card and shoved it in his pocket. Gran took a twenty-pound note from her purse and waited for the change. Joe took a pound coin off Gran's hand and gave it to the taxi driver for a tip. He knew taxi drivers expected one because he'd seen Mum, even in a state of emergency, give one to a taxi driver. The day he'd fallen off his bike and gashed his leg very badly. Mum couldn't stop the bleeding and so she wrapped a towel around his leg and phoned for a taxi. By the time they got to the hospital the towel was bright red with his blood. And even though he was bleeding all over the place, Mum made sure she did the right thing... she given a tip... so it was only right that he should do the same.

'Last of the big spenders, thanks lad,' said the driver as he took the coin. 'Thanks a lot. Don't forget to call if you need help and with that the driver jumped back inside and sped away.

# Chapter 22

Joe walked over to the big wrought iron gates to the caravan park and gave them a push and a pull which made them rattle. They shifted but wouldn't open. A big rusty chain and a padlock was keeping them tightly closed together.

'I'll walk down here and see if there's another way in. You wait here, Gran.'

'All right, Joe. I won't move. I'll stay put. Promise I will.'

Joe sprinted past the gates and along the fence. Further down, the fence had been trampled down almost flat and now it was so low that walking over the chicken wire was easy. Joe ran back to Granny Sal.

'The fence is broken a way down there. We can get over it no problem. Looks like a car has driven over it. Follow me, Gran.'

He picked up his bag, Mr Percival and his rucksack. Granny Sal pulled the trolley behind her. He would come back for the shopping bags later.

Joe climbed over the flattened fence and then helped Granny Sal over too. They lifted the trolley over together. Once they reached the road, Joe looked around. The sea was at the bottom of the hill and caravans dotted all over the field down to it. There must be hundreds of them.

'Now, the gates are behind us. Granddad used to drive…'

'Yes,' said Gran, 'he used to drive through the gates and carry on a long windy road and Tropical Sunset was over there on the right down towards the sea. It's in a lovely position. A short step down to the beach.'

'Can you try a bit harder, Gran. Can you remember exactly where it is because I can't?'

'I can't either at the moment. Now let me think. Granddad always knew where to go. I didn't take much notice.'

The road snaked off past the gates in different directions down to the sea. It was quite dark now and it was lucky the moon was out because that was the only light. If Gran could not remember then they would take hours to find the right one, all night probably. Joe's heart sank at the thought of having to look at every caravan to find the right one. And reading the names on all the caravans would be very difficult. If only he had thought to bring a torch. There was one in the cupboard under the stairs at home — he should have remembered it.

'Now let me see,' said Granny Sal sounding a bit doubtful that she could remember exactly where the caravan was. 'It's a while since I was here, Joe.'

'Yes, I know Gran but it's late and we must get ourselves sorted. Are you feeling cold?' said Joe.

'Yes, a little Joe. Now let me think… row seven, caravan five on the right rings a bell. Yes, Joe that was it.'

'Are you sure?' asked Joe thinking he would double check.

'Yes, Joe. Row six, caravan four.'

'You said row seven, caravan five last time,' said Joe realising that this could be a very long night. He was so tired that he could fall down on the ground and go to sleep. Last night he had not slept well. He had to take control. A decision had to be made, so he said…

'I'll go and have a look at both row six and seven. It must be in one of those. Don't move from here.'

'It's bound to be one of those and I won't move, Joe. Promise.'

'Good. Won't be long,' said Joe.

The clouds parted and the moon thankfully shone out and he found a signpost at the end of the first row and then found the one that said the number six, seven was the next one along. The fourth caravan on the right was called Tw-ig-let so that was not the one. He ran back to the crossroads where all the signposts were and headed off to row seven and found the fifth caravan. It was called something beginning with M. Mi-ll-eni-mum — he didn't waste too much time on it. That name was nothing like Tropical Sunset. Desperate now, he ran back to Gran.

'No, it's not either of those rows or numbers. Gran this is serious. We must find the right one. Think really hard.

Granddad must have told you hundreds of times.'

'Let me think. What was that little song he used to sing? Hang on a minute I think it's coming back to me. He used to sing it to the Happy Birthday song. You know the one we sing when you blow out your candles.'

Joe stared at Gran willing her to say something. He hopped from foot to foot. Then suddenly Gran started to sing,

*'Tropical Sunset's by the sea,*
*Its number is three,*
*It's down row two*
*And the door's painted blue.'*

'Well done, Gran,' thinking where did she get row six and seven from. It was nowhere near it.

Joe scuttled off to row two and found the third caravan and sure enough there was the name by the door... Tr-opi-ca-l S-u-n-s-e-t, he could just make out the name in the moonlight. As he turned to run back to Gran, he noticed a feint light shining through the badly fitting curtains of the caravan opposite. Funny that someone else was staying at the caravan park too. Perhaps they were the people that had driven over the fence to get into the caravan park. He wondered what they were doing here but he didn't wonder for long because he needed to get Gran safely into Tropical

Sunset and make her a cup of tea. When he reached Gran, he picked up his bag and Mr Percival's cage and said,

'Found it. Granddad's song worked. Come on Gran. This way.'

'Poor old Granddad. I miss him terribly, Joe.'

'I know you do, Gran. Come on we'll be fine. I'll look after you. There's nothing to worry about. Let's get ourselves sorted. And anyway, I'm starving.'

# Chapter 23

Gran rustled around in the bottom of her handbag and found the keys to Tropical Sunset and gave them to Joe. He climbed up the four wooden steps to the front door and pushed the key in the keyhole and twisted. It was very stiff and his hands were so cold he could not turn the key. He blew warm breath into his cupped hands and tried again. The key grudgingly turned very slowly. He pulled down the handle and the door swung open and a damp musty smell hit Joe's nose. It was just as freezing inside the caravan as it was outside.

Joe flicked light switch to on. Nothing happened.

'I'll have to turn the power on, Joe. I know what to do. I expect it will need some fifty pences for the meter.'

Gran went to the back of the caravan to a big free-standing box with a load of black wires sticking out of it that disappeared in through holes in the wall of the caravan, and pulled down a big handle.

'That's the power on now, Joe. We'll have to put some money in the meter now and then Bob's your uncle.'

'Who's Uncle Bob? I haven't got an uncle called Bob. I haven't got an uncle come to think of it,' said Joe.

'It's just a saying, lovey. Granddad was always saying it. It means, *it'll be fine.*'

Gran climbed the steps up to the caravan and stumbled her

way to the meter in the little kitchen. Joe found a fifty pence piece in his pocket and Gran pushed it into the meter and turned the dial. Joe flicked the light switch again and the caravan was suddenly full of light.

'I'll go back for the shopping, Gran.'

'OK love, I'll put the heaters on and get this place warmed up. It will be nice and cosy when you get back.'

Joe ran back to where the taxi had dropped them and picked up the shopping bags which he then lugged all the way back to the caravan. When he returned, he unpacked the shopping and found a place for everything in the fridge and the cupboards in the kitchen.

'I'll go and check the beds, Joe, and make them up. There's some hot water bottles in the cupboard over there,' she said pointing to a cupboard above the stove. 'We can fill them up with boiling water and put them in the beds. That will help to warm them up. There's a heater up the other end by the dining table you can put it on too and I'll put the ones on in the bedrooms. We'll have this place lovely and cosy in no time you'll see.'

Joe looked around and spotted the heater on the wall above the fold down table and the telly. Two benches were on either side of the table. He walked down to the heater and turned it on. He immediately got a smell of burning as the heat billowed out, but within a few seconds the smell went away. He closed all the curtains because they always did that at home in the winter to keep the warm in. He opened a door up the other end and found a funny looking loo with a red handle, but there was no bath or shower. Next there was a small cupboard with some hangers. Joe looked into the first bedroom and saw Granny Sal making up the bed. She seemed very much at home here. He knew she and Granddad spent a lot of time here together once he had retired. But she hadn't been back since he died.

'I'll put the kettle on,' said Joe.

'Good boy, but you'll have to go to the shower block for water, Joe. It's just at the end of the row where we came down. We're lucky we're so near because that's where we have to have a shower. But they'll be no hot water at the moment so we'll have to wash with boiled water in the sink for now,' said Gran disappearing under a Mickey Mouse duvet cover. 'You have to fill up the tanks to use the loo and the sink,' came another muffled answer.

Joe found a big, blue plastic jug in the cupboard under the sink and went outside in search of the shower block. He did remember seeing a brick-built building as he and Gran had walked down the path and he wondered what it was… now he knew.

It was very dark outside. Much darker than at home where the street lights blazed out and all the houses had their lights on. Here it was jet black and really spooky. But the night sky was beautiful and he gazed at all the stars and the big full moon which was helping him see his way. He had never seen so many stars back home. There must be more stars in the sky in the countryside. He'd love to go up in a rocket. What must it be like to go into space and see the stars from closer up there? He'd like to be like that astronaut he'd seen on the telly. That nice man with red hair, who looked a bit like his friend Mikey — what was his name? As he walked along, he tried to remember. What's-his-name had done a spacewalk too. He heard him talk about it. He'd like to see the earth from space like he did. How cool would that be? It must be brilliant. He wondered how difficult it would be to be an astronaut — would he have to go to university and train to be one or was there some other way? He didn't have a clue but he could *Google* it when he got back to school. How to be an astronaut — he knew *Google* would have the answers. I mean it couldn't be that difficult, could it? He would give this idea serious consideration if the Man U apprentice, police detective, being a pilot or a farmer did not work out. Oh yes, and he learnt to read.

There were funny noises too here in the countryside. Noises he could not identify. Then out of nowhere a big white bird silently flew towards him and just before he got to him, he swooped away but by that time Joe dodged him and fell to the ground his heart pounding. What on earth was that? Whatever it was, it was enormous. He was not sure whether there were vultures out here. He should have listened better in Miss Allcot's science lessons when they did a project on birds. One thing he did remember was that some birds really did pick up stuff in their talons and fly away with them. That bird was so big he might have seen him as prey and taken him to his nest and picked bits off him while he was still alive. Perhaps it was a prehistorical bird that was living here and had not been spotted until now and wasn't extinct. What if he'd discovered a new type of prehistoric flying dinosaur? He would try to get in touch with that old man from the telly that did the nature programmes and tell him what he had seen. He might even become famous too for finding a bird from the Jurassic period that everyone thought was extinct fifty million years ago.

Joe reached the shower block but it looked very dark and spooky. He listened at the door for any sounds and sure enough he could hear water dripping inside. He called out,

'Hello, it's only me, Joe.'

Hoping that if anything was inside, they would run off before he walked in, he took a step inside. Nothing happened. He ran his hand down the wall just inside the door and found a light switch and flicked it down but no light came on. As his eyes got used to the dark, he could see some taps ahead.

He rushed in, put the jug under the tap in the sink and turned the tap on. Water gushed out and when it was full, he lifted it up and trudged back with the heavy jug to Tropical Sunset.

Joe filled the kettle and put the rest of the jug of water on the floor in the kitchen. He struck one of Gran's matches, lit the gas ring and put the kettle over the flame.

'There you are, Joe. Thanks for getting the water. I'm dying for a cuppa. Can you give Mr Percival some water and some of his food and I'll open this can of tomato soup for our tea? We'll have to make that do. I'm worn out.'

'That's fine, Gran,' said Joe filling up Mr Percival's water tray from the jug. 'I'm tired too.'

'We'll have this and some bread. Then Swiss roll and a cup of tea. How does that sound?' asked Granny Sal.

'Yummy, I'm starving. The soup will help us warm up. The heaters are good,' said Joe.

'Those heaters are good. They work really quickly. Granddad bought them.'

'Here you are Mr Percival have some bird seed,' said Joe filling his bowl and topping up his water.

Mr Percival was sitting on his perch. When Joe filled his bowl to the brim he plopped down to the bottom of his cage and dipped his beak in the bowl and started to munch.

Joe laid the table and Granny Sal poured the hot soup into two bowls. Joe carried the plate of buttered bread to the table and two mugs of tea. When they had finished eating, they did the washing up with the rest of the boiled water left over in the kettle from when they made the tea and filled up the kettle again for the hot water bottles. Joe locked the caravan door and left the key on a hook by the sink. Then he pulled the pantaloons back over Mr Percival's cage and turned the heater down low and made sure there was nothing near that could catch fire.

When he had checked everything and checked it again just to make sure, it suddenly struck him that he had not spoken to Mum since yesterday. She would be worried he knew she would, but he had not seen a working phone box all day today. It had been a close shave seeing the police again. This place was so far off the beaten track they would be fine here. No one would think of looking for them here. He felt sure about that.

'I'll phone Mum tomorrow now we're here and let her know we're OK,' called Joe.

'That's right, Joe,' said Gran from her bedroom. 'She must be worried she hasn't heard. Night, love.'

'Night, Gran.'

Joe went into his room and quickly jumped into bed with all his clothes on. He had forgotten to bring pyjamas but it was so cold, there was no way he could have changed into them anyway. He pulled the duvet with the Mickey Mouse cover right up under his nose. The bed felt damp and chilly but the hot water bottle was lovely and cosy on his tummy and then he put it on his toes. He flicked the switch to off on the bedside light and was immediately plunged into darkness. If only he had his blue lantern with him. The one on his bedside cupboard at home. He had it on every night since he was a baby and now, he couldn't sleep without it. He lay staring at the ceiling but all could see was blackness. He imagined all sort of spiders coming down to attack him on their silken threads. He had even forgotten to check under the bed for monsters and mad scientists. He was too tired and too cold to get out of bed to see. He turned over on his side. He could hear scuffling sounds outside and the hoot from an owl but apart from that it was so quiet. He missed the sounds of cars going up and down the street and the people singing as they walked home from the Dog and Duck pub on the corner. And most of all he missed Mum. She always made everything seem fine but she wasn't here to sort them out. The job of keeping Gran safe from the police was a tough mission. His hardest yet in his role of "man of the house". He closed his eyes and thought about phoning Mum in the morning. He had to find a phone box and with that, he drifted off into a deep sleep.

# Chapter 24

*'The Police are concerned about the whereabouts of Sally Grimshaw aged sixty-five and her grandson, Joe Dawson aged eight who were last seen on Wednesday afternoon at Handby Station.'*

Marilyn was huddled under a blanket in the front room watching the New on the telly. There was Granny Sal and Joe's picture on the local news report.

*'They left a note to say they were travelling to Scotland but there has been no sighting of them getting on a train or plane going North. One useful other piece of information, they have their pet parrot with them. His name is Mr Percival. Anyone who has seen them or anyone who has any information concerning their whereabouts, should contact the Handby Police on 016998 275890.'*

Marilyn could not believe that this was happening to her. Where could they be? Why had Joe not called her? How could he be so thoughtless and worry her like this? As she walked out to the kitchen, she saw a photo on the wall of her, Joe and Granny Sal together in the park. They were all such good friends and Marilyn knew that Joe would do his best to take care of them both but he was such a little boy and there were so many dangers everywhere.

*\*\**

Joe was woken up by seagulls squawking outside and something was pounding across the roof of Tropical Sunset. What on earth was it? Maybe the dinosaur bird had come to find him and had great, big boots on. He looked out of the window and couldn't see anything. He would go outside as soon as he could and find out who the culprit was and hoped he was still there and ask him not to do it again or at least take his boots off. He stretched and felt stiff all over and when he breathed out little puffs of white cloudy stuff came out. The hot water bottle was now stone cold and there was ice on the inside of the window by the side of the bed. His nose felt so numb that he put his face under the duvet and did big breaths trying to defrost it.

Joe got out of bed and wrapped the duvet around him. There would be no shower or bath today. He'd just wash his face in some water and that would have to do. He was sure, in the circumstances Mum wouldn't mind this once. But there would be no hot water though until he put the kettle on the stove. You couldn't just turn on the tap in a caravan. Caravan holidays were definitely hard work. He switched on the light in the kitchen and it didn't come on. He could hear Granny Sal and seconds later she appeared wearing her coat and hat.

'Morning Joe. Goodness it's cold out here.'

'Morning. There's no electricity Gran.'

'We need some fifty pences to put in the meter. Have you got some more Joe?' asked Gran blowing breaths into her hands to try to get them warm.

Joe looked in the pocket of his trousers. He found a few ten pences and a couple of fives. 'I haven't,' he replied. 'Have you got any in your purse?'

Granny Sal rummaged around in her bag and found her purse. She shook her head. 'I haven't got any either.'

'I'll have to go and find a shop or a garage and get some change. Is there a shop nearby?'

'I think there's one quite near. Granddad used to walk there, Joe, every morning to get the paper and the milk. He said he liked the exercise. Why did I not think of getting the change before? Silly me,' said Granny Sal. 'I also remembered something last night as I was nodding off. I remember granddad saying something about his savings, Joe. He didn't keep it in the bank he kept it…'

'I better go out now and get some change,' said Joe not really listening, thinking what a twit he had been not to get the fifty pences for the meter.

'There be trouble afoot,' squawked Mr Percival hinting that he was still here and they hadn't fed him yet.

Joe set off leaving Granny Sal behind. He could go quicker by himself. He would look for a phone box too and phone Mum. He was dreading the call. He should have made more effort yesterday to call her but he really had not seen a phone box anywhere. All the time he had had to concentrate on trying to dodge the police and that was tricky. They had been lucky so far but he guessed Mum would not be pleased that he had skipped school to take Granny Sal off to goodness knows where to see some old friend she had never even heard of.

Joe walked up the lane. At the top there was a sign to Dr-ump-ton-on-the Pidd-le. He sounded the words out and they sounded a bit funny but this was the countryside and things were probably different out here. The sign also said one mile. Joe turned left and started to trot so he could get there a bit quicker. He was hungry and he knew Gran was gasping for a cup of tea. Further along the lane he heard what sounded like a car. It shot passed him leaving a cloud of dust. If only he was old enough to drive. He could have driven to the shop in no time at all.

After a little while, he came to a row of houses and in the middle was a pub with sign outside swinging from a post. The sign said, The Ripp-ling Pidd-le, and there was a painting of a river. Joe sounded out the words again wondering what a "piddle" could be. Everything around here seemed to have something to do with piddling — he was sure he'd read it sort of right but it could be paddling or puddling… but that didn't sound right either.

Further along the road he spotted a board outside what looked like another house and as he approached it, he saw it was an advert for ice cream. It must be a shop. It was. He read the name — Pidd-le  St-ore — no surprise there. Joe went in and picked up a carton of milk from the fridge and a newspaper. He handed the lady a ten-pound note.

'Could I have some fifty pences in the change please?' he asked.

The lady looked at him and smiled, 'Need them for the meter do you son?' she said.

'Yes, my nan needs them,' he said hoping his face was not going red.

'You're new to these parts. We don't get many visitors in November. Where are you staying?' enquired the lady.

Joe had to think quickly. Why was he there? Why are people so nosey? Why can't they mind their own business?

'We are just passing through,' said Joe quickly. He collected up his change and headed for the door. 'Is there a phone box anywhere?' he asked as he reached the door.

'Yes, there's one at the junction next to the beach.'

'Thank you,' said Joe politely and he dashed out before she could ask him anything else.

Joe walked to the crossroads and there was the phone box. He opened the door and it looked fine with no dangling or frayed wires. He picked up the receiver and heard the dialling tone. He put ten pence in the slot and dialled his home phone number. It started to ring. After three rings he heard.

'Joe, is that you?'

'Yes, Mum.'

'Where are you? I have been frantic with worry. I have the police out looking for you.'

'The police?' shouted Joe down the phone. 'Oh, mum why did you do that?'

'I had to do something to find you. You were on the News at Ten.'

'Now everyone knows what we look like. Mum how could you?' said Joe staring out of the telephone box windows. They were bound to be found now.

'Where's Granny Sal?' asked Mum. 'Is she there with you?'

'She's fine. We'll be home in a few days. Tell the police to call off the search. Bye.'

'Joe, Joe, where are you? Come home this minute. What about school?' she screamed down the phone.

But all she heard was a seagull screeching and a click.

# Chapter 25

As Joe turned back towards the caravan park, he noticed a police car outside the pub. It was white with fluorescent blue and yellow stripes all down the side. A policeman was standing outside talking to a man who was pointing in the direction of the caravan park. Joe turned around. He couldn't be seen. The police had found out where they were hiding. It was only a matter of time until their arrest. He waited behind the sea wall and soon enough the policeman got into the car and drove off and man went back inside the pub he popped his head up.

Joe dashed down the road as fast as he could even though he got a painful stitch in his side, until he reached the lane to the caravan park. He was panicking now. Mum had said they were on the telly last night. The lady in the shop must have missed the News or she would surely have recognised him. Perhaps she *did* recognise him and was phoning the police this very second to inform them of his whereabouts. He could feel the fifty pences jangling in his pocket. He carried on down the lane to Tropical Sunset. It would be risky to go out too much now but there was hardly anyone about. And what about the taxi driver? He was bound to phone the police if he had seen them on the News. He could identify them. Confirm it was them. He had wanted them to stay in the B and B and they had refused. He had only given him a quid for a tip. He would want to get his own back. He would shop them for sure.

Gran was waiting for him at the door of the caravan.

'I filled up the jug with water in the shower block for us so there's plenty.'

'I've got lots of fifty pences, Gran. I'll put a few in the meter.'

Joe filled up the metre. Gran put the kettle on, he told her about the phone call.

'I knew she would be worried, but telling the police. She always was a drama queen your mum. And we've been on the telly? What do you think of that Mr Percival? Fame at my age. Joe put the telly on.' Granny Sal flicked through the pages of the newspaper. 'Oh, look Joe. There's a report about us on page two. That's a nice photo of us. I am so glad mum chose a nice snap. Look Mr Percival. There's one of you too. Fancy that.'

Mr Percival swung on his perch looking at his picture and for once said nothing.

'Listen to this, Joe… The police are looking for two missing persons. An elderly lady and her grandson. Mrs Dawson, Joe Dawson's mother, told police that they left a note saying they were going to Scotland to visit a sick friend but so far there were no sightings of them. The stations and the airports are being watched. Anyone seeing these two people, Mrs Sally Grimshaw sixty-five, Joe Dawson eight and a parrot called Mr Percival are asked to get in touch with Handby Police on police on 016998 275890.'

'Gran this is serious. The police must be closing in. They must be looking everywhere for us not just in Scotland. There was a police car in the village where I got the change and the policeman was talking to a man outside the pub and he was pointing in this direction. Maybe they had insider information and they knew we were coming here. That was how they knew we were on the train and the ferry. But if that is the case, why don't they come and get us? It is pretty odd. I told mum we are in Scotland and I think she believed me so I think that will put them off the scent and we'll be fine for a few days. The police will search for us in Scotland and they'll never think of looking here for us. After breakfast would you like to have a walk by the sea?'

'That would be lovely Joe. Blow the old cobwebs away. That's what granddad used to say.'

'There be a force eight,' said Mr Percival.

*** 

It was a lovely day. That is, it was not raining. It was bitterly cold but there was a blue sky at least. Joe and Gran walked along the path at the side of the sandy beach. The seagulls were diving in and out of the waves and a little fishing boat chugged along dragging the fishing nets behind it. Joe looked out at the boat. It looked like great fun. He could see the fisherman driving the boat. The man waved and Granny Sal waved back. Joe thought that being a fisherman looked like a good job. All alone in the sea driving a boat. That was better than working in a shop or in an office which sounded really boring. Well, if he could not be a footballer, a pilot, a farmer or an astronaut he could try fishing. All that fresh fish for dinner. Mind you he only liked fish fingers because they did not have bones. Anyway, he would keep the idea in the back of his mind just in case he needed it.

# Chapter 26

Marilyn put the phone down. She was furious with Joe. How could he do such a thing? Running off to Scotland on some wild goose chase with Gran. Granny Sal was a terrible influence on Joe so she really blamed her. She gave him all the wrong food filling him up with stodge and sweets, gave him money all the time even when it was not birthdays and Christmas and let him stay up late watching all those old black and white films she loved when he should have been in bed. No wonder he was so terrible at reading and spelling. He was always half asleep the day after he stayed with her. Mr Taylor, the Headmaster, had told her Joe sat yawning some days in class at Parents Evening…

'Officer that was funny,' said Marilyn to the police lady who was sitting with her in the front room sipping a cuppa. 'I heard a seagull.'

'Yes, it was rather odd,' the police lady replied. 'I heard it too and the call came from the south coast on the Isle of Gull — not Scotland.'

'I have a feeling I know where they might be,' said Marilyn. 'Fancy at day out at Clarkson-on-Sea on the Isle of Gull? I think that's where they are.'

\*\*\*

It was dark already and Joe checked the time on his watch. It was only 3:45. The time went really slowly in the country. He was feeling really bored. He switched on the telly but there was only some programme about old stuff being fixed until it looked like new and a man asking people questions which they kept getting wrong.

All afternoon Granny Sal and him had played three games of *Snap* with a dog-eared pack of cards and a game of *Scrabble* but neither of them could spell the words so they gave up. Granny Sal had shown him how to play *Patience* but he got bored with that too. Granny Sal had gone to have a lie down because she said all this escaping from the police was too much for her old bones. He could hear her snoring in the bedroom.

He pulled the curtain back a bit and stared out of the window but all he could see was his refection. He was beginning to think that school was not so bad after all. And today was Thursday the best day of the week — there was football practice at lunchtime and art all afternoon. Thursday was usually sausages, beans and chips for lunch and probably apple pie and custard for pudding. Then there was the weekend with football training on Sunday with the school C team. He needed that session to practise being in goal. But here he was in a freezing cold caravan with nothing to do but play cards, watch rubbish telly that only old ladies watched, and look after his Granny Sal. He was worried about her because she was so old and a bit frail. It was a big responsibility looking after your Gran he knew that even better now. But he couldn't let her go to jail and he did not want to end up behind bars either.

He saw a car's headlights coming down the road. As quickly as he could, he let the curtain go, reached up and switched off the light. The car stopped outside. It must be the police. He pulled the curtain back a little bit. It was so dark it couldn't see but he could hear a scuffling sound coming from outside the caravan. He heard a car doors slam.

'Home sweet home,' said a deep voice.'

'Be quiet, Marty,' came a lady's voice.

'Garry, we forgot the sugar,' said the deep voice again.

'Then you'll have to do without,' said the lady.

'You're a hard woman, Nora,' said the deep voice.

'Shut up can't you,' came a reply.

Joe listened straining his ears. They must be staying in the caravan with the lights on he'd seen yesterday. Joe heard some steps. Then he heard the door bang. A flickering light appeared and he could see the peoples' shadows as they moved around. They must have a torch. Why couldn't they put the light on? Perhaps they forgot to get the sugar *and* the fifty pences for the meter too. He crawled on all fours to the bedroom and nudged Granny Sal.

'Gran, there are people in the caravan just up from us. I wonder why they're here. They must be hiding out here like us. Best not make a sound. We don't want them coming around asking questions do we,' said Joe in a whisper.

'What have they got to do with us, Joe? It's none of their business if we are here. Turn on the light and switch on the telly. Let's watch the six o'clock news. I'll put the kettle on. Those people are probably having a little holiday, Joe. They won't bother us,' said Granny Sal struggling to get up. 'The damp is not doing my arthritis any good, Joe.'

'Yes, I suppose you are right. They won't be interested in us, will they? The only thing is if they recognise us, they may report us to the police.'

'That's a chance we will have to take. I want a cup of tea and you must be starving. I'll put some sausages on. We'll have to have bags of crisps and pretend they are chips and I'll open a tin of beans. We can have the rest of the Swiss roll.'

Joe put the telly on to watch the six o'clock news...


*'The notorious, Turkey Shed Gang, who were connected with a bank raid two years ago in Lampton and have been spotted by an eyewitness in the vicinity of the ferries to the Isle of Gull. They are known as The Turkey Shed Gang because the local constabulary discovered their gang headquarters in an old turkey shed by the side of the A 6698*

*slip road. Police spokesman, Detective Morton, has advised that no one should approach them. They are also wanted for the bank raid on Western Bank in Handby on November 2^{nd} when £150,000 pounds was stolen at gun point. The gang members are known as Garry the Gorilla Buckman; forty-seven, Marty the Monster Cuthbert; thirty-five and the gang leader Notorious Nora Lovett aged sixty-three. If you see these people don't approach them.'*

'Bring down the main sail there's a tempest a brewing,' squawked Mr Percival.

'Shhhh,' chorused Granny Sal and Joe together and for once he did.

The newsreader carried on telling the news and then the weatherman spoke about the weather. There was no mention of them. They were not on the local news either. Joe and Granny Sal huddled together.

'Gran that's the names of the people in the caravan opposite. They must be The Turkey Shed Gang.'

'Best lock the door good and tight, Joe. Make sure the windows are locked too. We won't open the door to anyone,' said Granny Sal. 'Early tomorrow morning we'll head off and phone Mum. I think we have tried hard enough to run away. I think we will just go home and face the consequences. I'll own up and do my sentence. We can't keep running. I've had enough, Joe.'

Joe looked at Granny Sal and he had to agree. They were both tired, fed up and hungry and now they had dangerous criminals just across the way.

'You're right, Gran. We'll go home tomorrow.'

Joe missed his Mum and his bed at home and perhaps he might even make football training on Sunday…

It was then that there was a bang, bang on the door. They both sat completely still. They both held their breath. Mr Percival stopped swinging on his swing. There was another bang, bang, bang but this time it was louder.

'Is there anyone there?' came a voice.

## Chapter 27

Joe looked at Granny Sal. Neither said a thing.

'The sun is over the yardarm,' said Mr Percival.

Joe and Granny Sal put their fingers to their lips and stared at him.

'I'll have a bottle of rum,' he whispered very quietly.

'I can hear you in there. I only want to borrow some sugar,' came a lady's voice.

'Better give them some, Joe,' said Granny Sal.

Joe turned the key in the door and it clicked. Then he pushed the handle down and pulled the door open — but only a little bit. He stuck his nose through the gap. An old, thin, very tall lady with long white hair stood on the top step grinning. Joe looked her up and down. She had red shiny shoes with pointy toes and the tallest heels he'd ever seen and a long furry coat. She smiled at him and he could see some of her teeth were missing and the rest of them didn't look like she'd brushed them in weeks. She put her hand on the door frame and the rings on every finger clanked against the wood and dozens of bangles jangled around her wrists when she moved.

'We thought there was someone in here,' she cackled. 'Could you spare us a cup of sugar? I can drink my tea without it but my two lads won't drink tea without at least three spoons each.'

'I'll get you some,' said Granny Sal. 'My Bert was the same. He could not drink his tea without sugar either. Come in. Are you having a lovely holiday?' she asked.

Joe stood still. Gran must have forgotten they were in hiding from the Turkey Shed Gang and the police… again.

'Oh yes! There's nothing more bracing than the south coast of the Isle of Gull in November. Is that your parrot?'

'Squawk,' said Mr Percival.

'Yes, that's Mr Percival. I inherited him recently from my neighbour. I can't quite remember her name. Now, what was it? It will come to me if I give myself a minute,' said Granny Sal opening a cupboard and searching for a cup.

'Mrs Taggett,' whispered Joe and then cleared his throat answering for her to get rid of this woman. He didn't like the look of her.

'That's it. Mrs Taggett, God rest her soul. Mr Percival speaks and everything,' said Granny Sal.

'He is very handsome,' said the lady.

'And who is this?' asked Notorious Nora looking at Joe.

'I'm Alastair and this is my grandmother, Edith. We are on holiday too,' said Joe hoping Gran wouldn't say anything but she was busy putting the sugar into a bowl and didn't hear.

He hurried over to Gran and took the bowl off her.

'There you are, Joe. For the lady,' said Gran smiling.

He handed the lady the bowl and opened the door. She must get the hint to go now. He just hoped she hadn't seen their picture in the newspaper or on the telly.

'There you are,' he said, 'can you leave the bowl on the top step when you have finished with it.'

'I'll do that,' said Notorious Nora. 'Thanks.'

With that she turned around and left. Joe closed the door behind her and locked it immediately.

After dinner, Joe got into bed with all his clothes on again. He could not be bothered to even take his fleece off but he did kick his shoes under the bed. He snuggled under the Mickey Mouse duvet cover and closed his eyes and cuddled the hot water bottle again which he had refilled with boiling water. He could hear Granny Sal shuffling about and then everything went quiet.

He felt a thud at the bottom of his bed. He heard a fluttering of feathers. It was Mr Percival. He had forgotten to lock him away and put the pantaloons over him. Granny Sal must have forgotten too. As his eyes got used to the dark, he could see Mr Percival's silhouette and he tucked his head under his wing and went to sleep. Joe was so tired he could not be bothered to catch him and put him back in the cage. He could sleep on the end of his bed, it was fine. Joe felt himself drift off to sleep. Seconds later the whole caravan was bathed in bright blue flashing lights.

'Come out with your hands up,' said a voice through a megaphone. Joe jumped out of his skin. They had been found. Granny Sal was a criminal and he was an accessory to the crime. They had been discovered and would be found guilty. No excuses would be heard or listened to. He had seen this sort of thing on that police programme he never missed. The criminals would come out of their hideouts with their hands up and be arrested. They would have hand cuffs put on their wrists and shoved into the back of a police car. What was Mum going to say? She'd go ballistic when she found out.

'Joe, there's a load of lights outside and someone speaking with a very loud voice.'

'I know, Gran. I think it's the police. I think they've found us.'

'I think you're right, love,' called Granny Sal from her bedroom.

'Put your coat back on. They want us outside and it will be cold out there.'

Joe got out of bed and waited for Gran to appear. He took the keys off the hook and pushed the key in the lock and turned it.

'Joe, it's me. Stay in the caravan.'

'That sounds like Mum,' said Joe with surprise.

'What's she doing here. Has she come to get us?'

'What's going on?' said Joe looking at Gran.

'This is the police. We know you are in there. Come out slowly with your hands up,' said a voice.

Joe peered through a gap in the curtains. He saw the police thumping on the caravan across the way. He saw the door open and Marty and Garry fell down the caravan's steps and made a run for it but two policemen chased after them. Notorious Nora came out with her hands above her head and was met by another plain clothes policeman but she pushed him away and taken by surprise he stumbled back and fell on the ground. Suddenly, there was a terrible thumping on the caravan door, then a crack and a sound of metal breaking. The door broke away from the hinge and Notorious Nora appeared red faced and breathless. She rushed in and slammed the broken door shut. Joe and Gran backed away.

'Don't move. If you hadn't been here none of this would have happened. We had the perfect hideaway and now it's all over because of you,' she snarled.

'But we are hiding too,' said Joe.

'Hiding from what you little fool?' she spat.

'Gran is on the run. She has the stolen money.'

'What stolen money? We have the one hundred and fifty thousand. What are you talking about?'

'Gran has the money from the bank. She did not mean to

take it she just picked it up. It was in a M&S carrier bag.'

'Shut it, you stupid little twit,' yelled Notorious Nora.

'The news reader said the police were looking for an old lady who had stolen the money and because Gran had all this money in a bag, we thought she had stolen it,' said Joe.

'I did it. Where would I get all that money from?' said Granny Sal.

'Well how do I know? Now what am I going to do?' said Notorious Nora trying to work out her next move.

'I think you ought to give yourself up,' said Joe. 'I don't think you can make a run for it now. The police are surrounding us.'

'I'm not going back to prison. I'm taking control. You are my hostages. Come here boy and you too,' she said to Gran.

Notorious Nora lunged forward and grabbed Joe by the arms. She pulled him backwards and put her hand across his mouth.

'Don't hurt my grandson,' shouted Granny Sal. 'You leave him alone.'

Ignoring Granny Sal, Notorious Nora shouted, 'I've got the boy. Now let me go and I'll release him. Just start up the car and I'll be on my way. I won't hurt the boy if I can go.'

'Come on now, Lovett,' called one of the policemen through the megaphone. 'You know we can't do that. Let the boy go and come out with your hands up.'

'Never. I'm not going to prison again.' She squeezed Joe even tighter. Joe gave a muffled scream.

'Let him go,' said Granny Sal quietly. 'He's a good boy our Joe. He's done nothing wrong.'

Mr Percival wandered out of Joe's bedroom. He toddled across the floor then he swooped up and flew across the caravan and landed on top of Notorious Nora's head.

'Agghhhh!' she screamed reaching up to get rid of Mr Percival waving her hands to get him off. As she let go of him, Joe ran over to Granny Sal who grabbed him and held him tight.

'Quickly,' yelled Joe, 'I'm free.'

The door flung open and two policemen charged inside. They grabbed Notorious Nora and Joe caught Mr Percival.

'Thank you, Mr Percival. I think you have saved the day!' said Joe.

'Make mine a pint,' Mr Percival replied.

## Chapter 28

The policeman opened the door and stepped out with Notorious Nora in hand cuffs. The area outside the caravan was ablaze with headlights and blue flashing lights from the top of the police cars. Notorious Nora was met by another policeman and shoved into the back of a police car.

'Joe, Mum, you can come out now,' said Mum.

Joe ran into Mum's arms.

'Am I pleased to see you,' he said.

'What do you think you are doing running away and lying about where you were? Anything could have happened. Joe, I will never forgive you.'

'Well, it was like this, Mum…' started Joe.

'I'm not quite sure why we are here,' said Granny Sal, 'I seem to have forgotten. Are we on holiday?'

'No, Mum. It's November. It's a bit too cold for a caravan holiday this time of year. Now you two, can you tell me why you were with a bunch of criminals at the sea-side in November?' said Marilyn.

'Well, it all started on Tuesday,' started Joe again.

\*\*\*

Joe sat opposite the police officers with Granny Sal and his

Mum sitting next to him. He had never been in a police station before. There was lots going on around him and it was all very exciting.

'Right son. So, on Tuesday. What exactly happened?'

'I went to Gran's after school for my tea and she showed me this big bag of money and she said she had been in the raid at the bank. These men with monster masks on had held up the bank. She said there was a bag by her on the floor and she just picked it up and taken it home. It was then that she realised that it did not belong to her and that she must have picked it up as the raiders escaped. Someone must have dropped the bag and she picked it up. She thought it belonged to the man in front of her in the queue. They said you were looking for an old lady in a hat. We thought it was Gran.'

'No, that was not possible,' said the policeman. 'The Turkey Shed Gang got away with all the money from the Western Bank raid in black bags. Notorious Nora wore a hat to disguise herself. She was in the queue with Gran. We've been following the gang ever since. We had a good description of their getaway car. Then they dumped the car and took the same train as you. We lost them and then we had a sighting of Notorious Nora. Then they must have split up and taken different ferries but Notorious Nora was on the same ferry as you. It was all such a coincidence.'

'I thought you were following us all the time,' said Joe. 'I saw the policemen on the train and the ferry and in the village. I thought they were trying to find us. I thought we would be on *Crimewatch* and there would be "Wanted Posters" everywhere. We thought we could hide out on the island. I did not want Granny Sal to go to prison.'

'There is no chance of that, son. The money your Granny Sal had was *her* money. She was going to deposit the money in her bank account. We found the paying in slip on the floor of the bank after the attempted raid. It is with all the other evidence in Handby Police Station. The old man in front of you, Mrs Grimshaw, was Arnold Accrington. We found his bag of money behind one of the displays in the bank. It must have got kicked there during the raid.'

'Was it *my* money in that bag?' said Gran. 'No, it can't have been.'

'It was, Mrs Grimshaw.'

'Oh, hang on a minute. Now let me think. Oh yes, I remember now. That is what I was trying to tell you, Joe. I thought Granddad took my advice and put his money in the bank. But when I did the hoovering, I moved the coffee table and I remembered the secret hiding place. When I looked inside it was full of cash. He'd stashed all his life savings in there even though I told him not to.'

'I think I know that now, Gran,' said Joe.

'I thought I better take it to the bank. Normally I take

money out on Wednesday for the house keeping but I was putting some in. Silly me. I must have forgot at the time.'

'It doesn't matter, Gran,' said Joe. 'Keep going. The police want to know what happened.'

'Then a while ago I heard your Mum say how much she would love a holiday and a little car would make life so much easier and I remembered the money he had hidden and I thought to myself... Sal get that money out and spend the lot. Put it in the bank where it will be safe and then do some good with it. I'm fed up with seeing my daughter trudge off to work on the bus. I thought a little car might make your life easier dear and there's enough for a holiday for you and Joe. Two weeks somewhere nice and hot. That was why I had the money. I did not steal it after all.'

'Well Gran we had an adventure,' was all Joe could think of saying.

'And it all sorted itself out in the end. You're the best grandson anyone could have Joe.'

'And you're the best Gran. But next time you go to the bank. I'm coming too.'

'What's eBay?' said Mr Percival.

'Something you don't need to worry about now my brave boy,' said Gran to Mr Percival. 'I couldn't possibly sell you now. You're a hero who saved us both. Isn't that right, Joe.'

And all Joe could think of saying was, 'Yes.'

# Author Bio

Ruth has been a teacher for a very long time. She loves being in the classroom making learning fun and specialises in teaching reading and spelling. Now retired, Ruth teaches children with learning difficulties at her home and it doesn't matter how old they are, she loves to help!

Ruth has always told stories to the children she teaches. Her book, The Turkey Shed Gang, is for 7–8-year-old independent readers. She also writes for dyslexic children in mind so that they can read a book, maybe with a little help, which is age appropriate for them.

When she's not teaching, Ruth loves walking in the Surrey Hills where she lives with her husband, who is a retired airline Captain. They take every chance to travel worldwide and it's on trips away that Ruth comes up with her ideas for her books, always scribbling notes down in her purple notebook which she carries everywhere.

Ruth loves baking bread and cakes and is always in the kitchen with her vast collection of cookery books. She has been interviewed by the BBC three times about writing, environmental issues and her work with dyslexic children, and had an article published in a national magazine for parents.

www.ruthyoung.co.uk

www.blossomspringpublishing.com

Printed in Great Britain
by Amazon